SHOWDOWN

Fargo's nerves were taut and ready for trouble. His keen hearing picked up the scrape of a foot and the metallic ratcheting of a gun being cocked. He pivoted swiftly, his left hand going out to shove Olmsted to the ground as his right swept down to the revolver at his hip. The Colt whispered out of gun leather as muzzle flame bloomed garishly orange in the darkness of an alley mouth beside the saloon.

Fargo heard the wind-rip of the bullet past his ear. The next instant the Colt bucked twice in his hand as he thumbed off a pair of shots and sent lead screaming into the alley. He dropped to a knee as he cocked the gun and fired again. More muzzle flashes split the shadows. Hoofbeats hammered into the night, coming closer. Fargo threw himself to the side as a horse loomed up and almost trampled him.

The rider was leading two horses with empty saddles. Fargo landed on his belly and loosed another round as two men hustled out of the alley and vaulted onto the riderless horses. They kicked the mounts into a gallop as they leaned far forward in the saddles, making smaller targets of themselves. . . .

THE TRAILSMAN
#276

SKELETON CANYON

by

Jon Sharpe

A SIGNET BOOK

SIGNET
Published by New American Library, a division of
Penguin Group (USA) Inc., 375 Hudson Street,
New York, New York 10014, U.S.A.
Penguin Books Ltd, 80 Strand,
London WC2R 0RL, England
Penguin Books Australia Ltd, 250 Camberwell Road,
Camberwell, Victoria 3124, Australia
Penguin Books Canada Ltd, 10 Alcorn Avenue,
Toronto, Ontario, Canada M4V 3B2
Penguin Books (NZ), cnr Airborne and Rosedale Roads,
Albany, Auckland 1310, New Zealand

Penguin Books Ltd, Registered Offices:
80 Strand, London WC2R 0RL, England

First published by Signet, an imprint of New American Library,
a division of Penguin Group (USA) Inc.

First Printing, October 2004
10 9 8 7 6 5 4 3 2 1

The first chapter of this book previously appeared in *Ozarks Onslaught*, the
two hundred seventy-fifth volume in this series.

Copyright © Penguin Group (USA) Inc., 2004
All rights reserved

 REGISTERED TRADEMARK—MARCA REGISTRADA

The Trailsman

Beginnings . . . they bend the tree and they mark the man. Skye Fargo was born when he was eighteen. Terror was his midwife, vengeance his first cry. Killing spawned Skye Fargo, ruthless, cold-blooded murder. Out of the acrid smoke of gunpowder still hanging in the air, he rose, cried out a promise never forgotten.

The Trailsman they began to call him all across the West: searcher, scout, hunter, the man who could see where others only looked, his skills for hire but not his soul, the man who lived each day to the fullest, yet trailed each tomorrow. Skye Fargo, the Trailsman, the seeker who could take the wildness of a land and the wanting of a woman and make them his own.

Arizona, 1860—
A rich, wild land where evil men
cast long shadows in the hot sun.

1

The big man in buckskins was coated with a thick layer of trail dust, as was the black-and-white Ovaro stallion he led along the street. Weariness lay heavily on both of them, but no amount of exhaustion could completely disguise the strength and vigor that was naturally theirs. Man and horse were both magnificent specimens, and under better circumstances that would be evident.

But right now they were plumb worn out after days on a long, hard trail, and all they wanted was rest.

The man, at least, was not destined to get it. Not right away, anyway.

His name was Skye Fargo. At the sound of a loud, angry voice, he raised his head and looked to the left, toward a saloon called the Pine Tree. A man came flying backward through the entrance, knocking aside the batwing doors. His booted feet flailed desperately as he tried to catch his balance on the wide boardwalk, but he failed in the effort and plunged off the edge into the street, to land with a resounding crash right in front of Fargo.

Fargo stopped and looked down at the man, as did the stallion. Fargo's gaze was one of curiosity, because his mind was always alert no matter how tired he was. The Ovaro, on the other hand, regarded the man lying in the dust with more of a baleful glare. This human, whoever he was, formed a barrier between the horse and its rightful rest.

The man on the ground blinked rheumy eyes, stared up at Fargo, and said, "Lord, you're a big one, ain't you?"

"Are you all right, old-timer?" Fargo asked.

The man, who was mostly bald, with a fringe of white hair that matched his tuft of white beard, pushed himself unsteadily to his feet. His leathery face showed the effects of years spent in sun and wind, in biting cold and blistering heat. His clothes were on the ragged side, but not too tattered. He swatted at them, raising clouds of dust, and said, "I'm fine, lad, don't worry about me."

He had a slight accent, probably British, Fargo thought. He had run into Englishmen on the frontier before. This big land drew all sorts, from all over the world.

Fargo slapped the man on the shoulder and started to lead the stallion around him. "All right, then. Better be more careful in the future."

"Oh, I intend to. No more fisticuffs for me." The old man turned toward the Pine Tree Saloon, and as he did so, he reached into the front of his shirt and pulled a gun that had been tucked into the waistband of his ragged trousers.

Fargo's lake-blue eyes narrowed. From the looks of it, the old-timer intended to burst back into the saloon and start blazing away at whoever had thrown him out. As Fargo got a better look at the gun in the light that spilled through the saloon's entrance, he revised his opinion. The revolver was ancient, rusted, and probably wouldn't fire.

But if the old man stomped in there and started waving it around, odds were that somebody would pull a working gun and let some daylight into his innards. Other people might get hit by stray bullets if lead started flying, too.

So even though this was really none of his business,

Fargo sighed, reached out, and caught hold of the old man's sleeve.

"Wait a minute," Fargo said. "You don't want to go in there like that."

"The hell I don't." The old man tried unsuccessfully to tug his sleeve loose from Fargo's grip. "A feller's got to defend his honor, don't you know?"

"Getting killed is no way to do it."

The old-timer turned an owlish gaze toward Fargo. "Sometimes it's the only way," he said softly.

Fargo might have continued the argument, but at that moment, heavy footsteps from the boardwalk made him glance in that direction. A tall, massively built man with broad shoulders and long arms seemingly as thick as tree trunks had slapped the batwings open and stepped out of the saloon. He had an ugly, rawboned face and a tangle of coppery hair under a pushed-back black hat. He hooked his thumbs in the gun belt strapped around his hips and said, "How come you're just standin' there, you damned old pelican? Didn't I tell you to drag your ass outta Gila City?"

The old man's eyes widened even more. He started to jerk the useless old revolver upward, but he was slow about it, more than slow enough to get himself killed. The man on the boardwalk cursed and grabbed for his own iron.

Fargo left his feet in a flying tackle.

He crashed into the old man and bore him to the ground as a gun roared. The slug spanked through the space where the old-timer's head had been a split second earlier. Fargo rolled over and surged up into a crouch. He held his left hand toward the man on the boardwalk, palm out, as he shouted, "Hold your fire!" His right hand hovered close to the butt of the Colt on his hip just in case the man tried to trigger another shot.

The man on the boardwalk let the barrel of his gun drop a little. Smoke curled from the muzzle. "What

3

in blue blazes are you doin', mister?" he yelled at Fargo. "You could'a got yourself killed!"

"Nobody needs to get killed over this," Fargo said. "Just take it easy."

The man on the boardwalk snorted in contempt. "Tell that to that worthless old bum whose hide you just saved. He's the one who pulled iron on me."

Fargo reached down and picked up the revolver the old man had dropped. "You couldn't hammer a nail with this thing without it falling apart, let alone shoot anybody."

"Well, how in hell was I supposed to know that? All I saw was somebody tryin' to point a gun at me!"

The man had a point, Fargo thought. The old-timer was at least partially to blame for this ruckus.

"All right, you know now you don't have anything to worry about. Why don't you holster that hogleg and go back inside?"

"You gonna get that stinkin' old man out of here?"

"If that's what it takes," Fargo said.

The man shrugged and slid his gun back in its holster. "All right. But if I catch sight of him again tonight, I'm liable to beat him to death. Remember that."

Fargo didn't say anything, but he didn't think he was likely to forget the big redheaded man—or his threats.

The man went back into the Pine Tree. The rest of the saloon's patrons had crowded around the door and the windows, watching the confrontation, and they greeted him with cheers and backslaps as if he were some sort of conquering hero. Fargo just shook his head and reached down to help the old-timer to his feet.

"You didn't have to do that," the old man whined. "I don't need nobody to fight my battles."

"Then you should choose them more wisely," Fargo said. He picked up his wide-brimmed brown hat, which had fallen off when he tackled the old man,

4

slapped it against his thigh to get some of the dust off it, and put it back on his head. He wrapped his fingers around the old man's skinny upper arm. "Come on. You look like you could use something to eat, and so could I."

Actually, when he had reached Gila City, he had been thinking more of sleep than anything else, but he was willing to postpone that for a while. He steered the old man down the settlement's main street and a couple of blocks later found a hole-in-the-wall hash house that was still open. Fargo left the Ovaro at the hitch rail and took the old man inside.

The place had no tables, only crude stools along a counter made of rough-hewn planks. Fargo and the old man were the only customers. The proprietor was a middle-aged Chinese man who put burned steaks and scorched potatoes in front of Fargo and the old-timer without asking what they wanted, then added cups of steaming coffee. The food was pretty bad, but Fargo was hungry enough to eat it anyway. The coffee was a different story. In one of those rare instances of finding a diamond surrounded by trash, it was wonderful. Fargo felt some of his strength returning as he sipped the strong black brew.

"I appreciate this, lad," the old-timer said as he gnawed at the tough steak. "Things have been a bit lean and hungry in recent weeks." He put his fork down and extended a gnarled hand. "Bert Olmsted," he introduced himself.

Fargo shook with him. "Skye Fargo."

"It's pleased I am to make your acquaintance, Mr. Fargo. Or should I call you Skye?"

Fargo shrugged. "Whatever you like."

"Call you anything as long as it's not late to supper, eh?" Bert Olmsted slapped the counter and cackled. "You Yanks and your witticisms."

Fargo wasn't the one who had made the weak joke, but he let that pass. Olmsted might not be falling-down drunk, but it was obvious he had put away a considerable amount of Who-hit-John during the evening. Fargo thought the food and coffee might sober him up a little.

"Who was that fella who tossed you out of the Pine Tree?" Fargo asked when they had polished off the steak and potatoes.

"The miscreant's name is Flynn Pearsoll," Olmsted replied. "And a more belligerent sort I've never run across. All I did was ask him to perhaps stand me the cost of a drink, and he acted like a bull seeing red. Bellowed that I stank and threw me bodily out of the establishment." Olmsted sniffed. "I suppose I am a bit odoriferous, but still, there are limits."

"You shouldn't have pulled your gun."

"Yes, I suppose you're correct about that. By the way, might I have it back?"

Fargo had tucked the old revolver behind his belt. He took it out and slid it along the counter to Olmsted. "Is that thing even loaded?"

"Of course. What good is an unloaded gun?"

In this case, it probably didn't matter, but there was always a slight chance that the revolver might go off if it was loaded. "Better be careful with it," Fargo said. "It looks like it might blow up on you if you tried to fire it."

"Nonsense. It's a fine weapon." Olmsted looked Fargo up and down. "You're rather heavily armed yourself, my friend."

Fargo had the Colt on his hip and an Arkansas Toothpick in a fringed sheath strapped to his right calf. A Henry rifle rode in a saddle boot on the Ovaro outside.

Fargo drank the last of his coffee and said, "Man never knows when he's going to run into trouble."

"My motto, exactly!"

"Tell me more about Pearsoll," Fargo suggested. He hadn't really crossed swords with the man, so to speak, but he had the feeling Pearsoll might hold a

6

grudge because of the way Fargo had interfered in his clash with the old man.

Before Olmsted could say anything, the Chinese man behind the counter shook his head and said, "Flynn Pearsoll bad man. Drink half the time, fight half the time, chase ladies half the time."

"That's three halves," Fargo pointed out with a grin.

"There plenty of Pearsoll to go 'round."

"Yeah, from the looks of him I'd say you might be right."

"He's killed four men in Gila City and the vicinity," Olmsted said solemnly. "That we know of."

"Are you saying I'd better watch my back?"

Olmsted shrugged his bony shoulders. "Not your back, necessarily. Pearsoll, to give credit where credit is due, generally shoots his victims from the front. That is, when he doesn't thrash the life out of them. That's happened on at least one occasion."

"I'm not in the habit of walking around scared," Fargo said. "But I'll keep my eyes open."

The door of the hash house opened behind them. Fargo glanced over his shoulder, then looked again at the two newcomers who hurried into the place.

He would have taken a second look at the two young women no matter where they were. They were that pretty. But here in these squalid surroundings, their beauty seemed even more striking.

One was blond and blue-eyed, tall and slender with long, straight hair and a fair complexion. The other was shorter and more richly curved, with brown eyes and a mass of dark brown curls that tumbled around her shoulders. Both wore men's trousers that hugged their hips nicely, along with flannel shirts and floppy-brimmed felt hats. They should have been in ball gowns, Fargo thought, with a waltz playing somewhere.

"There you are, you bloody old fool," the brunette said.

7

"We heard you nearly got yourself killed," the blonde said. "Again."

Olmsted held up his hands. "Girls, girls," he said. "No need to come in here screeching at me like a pair of harridans."

Fargo didn't think the young women sounded like that at all. No doubt they were worried about the old-timer and probably more than a little frustrated with him, too. He had a feeling Bert Olmsted could try the patience of a saint. He also wondered what the women were doing in a rough-and-tumble mining town like Gila City, and what their connection was to the old man.

He found out the answers a moment later when Olmsted said, "Skye, I'd like for you to meet my granddaughters. The fair one is appropriately named Gloriana, while the dark-eyed beauty is Evangeline."

"Glory," the blonde snapped. "I never liked that highfalutin name."

"And I'm Vangie," the brunette said. She paid more attention to Fargo, running her brown-eyed gaze over his muscular form with an appealing boldness. "You must be the fella who saved Gramps from getting his lights put out permanent-like."

"I just tried to give him a hand," Fargo said.

"Well, we appreciate it," Glory said. She looked at Fargo, too, and seemed to like what she saw. "You don't know how big a job it is, keeping him out of trouble. We thought we could come into town for some supplies without any problems, but he wandered off."

"I told you where I was goin'," Olmsted protested.

Both young women shook their heads. "No," Vangie said. "You didn't. We looked up and you were gone."

Glory gave an unladylike snort. "Didn't take much thinking to figure out where you might be, though. We went down to the Pine Tree and heard that you got in some sort of fracas with Flynn Pearsoll."

8

Olmsted scowled down into his empty coffee cup. "The man's a rotter, an absolute rotter."

The proprietor of the hash house said, "Miss Glory, Miss Vangie, you want some coffee?"

"Thanks, Johnny," Glory said. "That would be nice."

She took a step toward the stool next to Fargo, but somehow Vangie got there first and settled her neat little rump on it. She gave Fargo a smile, ignoring the glare that Glory sent her way. Reluctantly, Glory went to sit on the other side of her grandfather.

Fargo said, "No offense, but you ladies don't look much like sisters."

"We're not," Vangie said. "We're cousins."

Glory leaned forward and said, "Her pa and my pa were brothers."

"Don't really sound English, either," Fargo commented.

Vangie snorted this time. "No reason we should."

"We were born and raised in New Mexico Territory," Glory put in.

Olmsted scratched his bald scalp. "You see, Skye, I came to your wonderful country at a rather young age. My children were born here, so naturally my grandchildren were, too."

"Reckon that makes us as American as anybody," Vangie said.

Fargo nodded in understanding. "From the looks of it, you've been doing a little prospecting?"

"We're going to find gold and make our fortune," Glory declared.

Olmsted made shushing motions with his hands. "Now, girls, don't go natterin' about such things. That's our own private business."

Fargo smiled and said, "Don't worry, I'm not interested in jumping anybody's claim."

"And I strike gold right here," Johnny put in from the other side of the counter.

Vangie looked curiously at Fargo and asked, "What

9

is your business in Gila City, if you don't mind my asking?"

"Don't mind at all," Fargo said. "I'm looking for a place to get some sleep, and then I reckon I'll push on to California."

"Where'd you come from?" Glory asked.

"I was over in Texas, place called El Paso. Got a letter from a friend in San Francisco that said he might have a job for me. Thought I'd ride out and see about it."

"What sort of work do you do?" That question came from Vangie.

"Scouting, mostly."

Vangie looked at him intently. "What did you say your name was?"

"Didn't say. It's Skye Fargo."

"I knew it! I thought Gramps called you Skye. You're the Trailsman."

Fargo inclined his head. "Some have called me that."

Glory leaned forward again. "Is he the one that—"

"He's the one," Vangie said.

Fargo didn't know what they were talking about. "Have we met before?" he asked. He thought it was unlikely he would forget two such attractive young women, but anything was possible.

"No, but we saw you over in Santa Fe one time, a year or two ago."

"I've been to Santa Fe," Fargo allowed.

"You were there doing some scouting for the army, I think."

"I remember saying you were a mighty handsome man," Glory added. "Never thought we'd meet you in person, though."

"Well, thanks," Fargo said. He knew women found him attractive and didn't dwell on the fact one way or the other. It didn't seem like anything worth spending a lot of time on. "I'm sorry I didn't make your acquaintance then."

"Oh, don't worry about that," Vangie said with a

wave of her hand. "Lord, that's a long, hot, dusty ride from El Paso to here."

"It is that," Fargo agreed.

"We'd better let you get on over to the hotel so you can rest," Glory said as she stood up from the stool. She took Olmsted's arm. "Come on, Gramps."

The old-timer had fallen into a half doze as his lovely granddaughters talked to Fargo. He jerked his head up and said, "Eh? Oh, I see. Time to call it a night, eh?"

"That's right, Gramps," Vangie said as she moved in and took his other arm. "Let's get back to the wagon."

"Are you going back to your camp tonight?" Fargo asked. Driving a wagon over this rugged corner of Arizona in the darkness didn't strike him as a very good idea.

"No, we'll wait until morning. Maybe we'll see you again before we go."

"Maybe," Fargo said. He touched the brim of his hat and nodded to the young women. "Good night, ladies."

They smiled at Fargo and then led Olmsted out of the eatery. When they were gone, Johnny sighed and said, "Miss Glory and Miss Vangie fine young ladies. But old Bert . . . he a pure-dee handful for them."

"I'll bet," Fargo agreed with a grin. He pulled out a leather poke and took some coins from it to pay for the food and coffee. Johnny grinned and swept the money off the counter.

"You come back for breakfast in the morning," he suggested. "Not as fancy as hotel dining room, but good food. And Miss Glory and Miss Vangie probably be here."

Fargo didn't mention the fact that Johnny's food would have to improve considerably to be mediocre. But the coffee was good and he wouldn't mind seeing Glory and Vangie again. He nodded to Johnny and said, "I'll see you in the morning."

*   *   *

Gila City had been in existence for only a couple of years, but like most settlements that came into being because of gold, it had grown quickly. Located on the Gila River just east of the spot where the stream merged with the larger Colorado River flowing down from the north, the town had several streets and dozens of buildings, one of which was a fairly decent hotel that had a stable behind it. Fargo rented a room and then settled the Ovaro in one of the stalls, giving the stallion plenty of grain and water. He carried his saddle and saddlebags up the stairs to the hotel's second floor, where his room was located.

After lighting the lamp, Fargo looked longingly at the bed for a moment. He wanted to stretch out, but he was so covered with dust that he didn't like the idea of lying down in it. With a sigh, he blew out the lamp and returned to the lobby.

"There a place around here I can get a bath?" he asked the clerk.

"At this time of night? I don't know, mister. There's a bathhouse down the street, but it may not be open this late. There's always the river, too, but there's patches of quicksand in the bed."

"I'll take a chance on the bathhouse," Fargo said. "Whereabouts would I find it?"

"Just the other side of the Pine Tree Saloon. You know where that is?"

Fargo nodded. "I know."

He left the hotel and walked along the street. Several saloons were still open, but the Pine Tree was the largest and the busiest. Raucous music and laughter floated into the night past the batwings. Fargo glanced in as he went past and saw Flynn Pearsoll standing at the bar knocking back a shot of whiskey. Several men hung around Pearsoll, drinking with him, and although they weren't as big as the redhead, they looked almost as tough. Fargo had seen such men before, plenty of them, and he figured they were no more honest than they had to be.

He wasn't looking for trouble, though, so he moved on. As long as Pearsoll didn't try to hurt Bert Olmsted again, Fargo would mind his own business.

The door of the bathhouse was open, and a light burned inside. Fargo stopped in the doorway and asked, "Are you still open?"

A stocky man with a thick mustache sat at a desk. Without looking up from the ledger where he was carefully scratching some figures with a pen, he said, "No hot water left, and I ain't of a mind to build up the fire again."

"I'll make do with cold, then," Fargo said. Anything to get some of the dust off of him.

"Your choice, mister. Tubs in the back. You'll find the water there, too, still on the stove."

Fargo nodded and walked past the desk. The rear part of the building had been divided into stalls with partitions between them that didn't reach all the way to the ceiling. Each stall contained a big wooden tub sealed with pitch. The water in most of the tubs was filthy from previous users, but Fargo found one that was empty. He got a bucket and filled the tub with water from the large vat that sat on a cast-iron stove. The stove was cold, the fire out for the night, but the water was still lukewarm. It would do.

Fargo unstrapped his gun belt and coiled it, placing it on a three-legged stool beside the tub along with the Arkansas Toothpick. He hung his hat on a nail driven into the partition. Then he took off his buckskins and shook them out the best he could. He wore the bottom half of a pair of long underwear underneath them. That came off and was shaken out as well.

Then Fargo stepped into the tub and lowered himself into the water. He held his breath and went all the way under for a moment. When he came up, water streamed through his thick black hair and dripped from his close-cropped beard. He leaned back, resting his arms on the sides of the tub. A long sigh came from him.

As tired as he was, it would have been easy for him to doze off as he sat in the tub. He fought off the drowsiness and started lazily scrubbing some of the dirt off his skin.

He looked up as footsteps and the jingling of spurs sounded from the front of the bathhouse. A harsh voice said, "Take a walk, Giddings."

"I'm workin' on my books," the owner of the place complained, a whine in his voice.

"Keep back-talkin' me and you'll have to enter a big loss in that ledger after this rattrap burns to the ground."

"All right, all right, take it easy, Flynn. I'm goin'."

Fargo had already recognized Flynn Pearsoll's voice. He didn't figure that the big hardcase's visit to the bathhouse boded any good, and a moment later he knew it.

"I know you're back there, mister," Pearsoll said. His words were slightly slurred. He was drunker than he had been earlier in the evening. "Might as well come on out and take what you got comin' to you. You never should've stuck up for that old coot. Now I've got to beat the hell out of you for meddlin' in my business."

Fargo knew what Pearsoll meant. Pearsoll had the citizens of Gila City scared of him, and that gave him power over them. But his grip on that power would begin to slip if anyone successfully stood up to him, as Fargo had earlier. Pearsoll had to show the town that he was still the big he-wolf of these parts, and the only way to do that was to destroy the man who had dared to defy to him.

Now, like it or not, worn out or not, Fargo had a fight in front of him.

2

Fargo stood up, letting the water sluice off him. Pearsoll, or one of his friends, must have seen him go by the saloon and then trailed him down here. As Fargo had suspected, Pearsoll felt like he had a score to settle with him. That feeling probably had been aggravated by the amount of whiskey Pearsoll had poured down his gullet.

As he stepped out of the tub, Fargo glanced down at the water. It was a lot dirtier than when he had gotten in. He would have liked to soak a while longer, but at least he had washed some of the sweat and trail dust off.

Of course, he was liable to get dirty again if he had to fight Pearsoll, but that couldn't be helped. Winning and staying alive were a lot more important.

He pulled on his underwear and the buckskin trousers, then buckled the gun belt around his waist. He left the Arkansas Toothpick on the chair. Barefooted, he stepped out of the stall formed by the partitions.

Pearsoll was cursing and demanding that Fargo come out. He stopped short as the Trailsman said calmly, "Looking for me?"

Pearsoll stood beside the bathhouse owner's desk. The owner was nowhere in sight, having scurried out when Pearsoll told him to go. A couple of the big redhead's friends lounged in the doorway, and through the window Fargo could see a couple more on the boardwalk outside.

"You!" Pearsoll exclaimed as he pointed a long, blunt finger at Fargo. "We got something to settle, you and me."

Fargo shook his head. "Not really. There's no trouble between us, and I don't see any reason to start some now."

"You stood up for that smelly old bastard!"

"All I did was keep him from getting killed."

"Well, I wanted to kill him!"

Fargo smiled faintly. "We don't always get what we want."

"I do, mister," Pearsoll said, lowering his voice. He was drunk, but not so much so that he wasn't dangerous. "I do."

Fargo had learned to watch everything about an enemy: his eyes, his hands, the way he held his body. He didn't think Pearsoll wanted a gunfight. Pearsoll wanted to thrash the living daylights out of Fargo with his bare hands. He was probably capable of breaking most of the men around here in half.

Fargo shook his head and said again, "I don't want trouble."

"You got it whether you want it or not. Unless you're nothin' but a damned coward. That what you are, mister? You want to go out there in the street and holler it out so the whole town can hear it? You do that and I might let you walk away."

"No thanks," Fargo said. "I don't believe I will."

Pearsoll's eyes narrowed. He didn't try to goad Fargo into action with any more insults. He didn't issue any more threats or declare what a big man he was. He just roared a curse and launched himself at Fargo, both fists swinging in hammerlike blows.

Fargo ducked under the punches, but he couldn't avoid Pearsoll's rush entirely. Pearsoll crashed into him and drove him backward. Fargo tried to brace himself, but his bare feet slipped on the damp floor. He felt himself falling.

Pearsoll was two or three inches taller and probably forty pounds heavier. If he landed on top, Fargo might not be able to dislodge him. Fargo twisted as he fell, trying to get out from under the bigger man. He succeeded, landing on his side as Pearsoll hit the floor facedown a few inches away.

Fargo rolled and came up smoothly. Pearsoll was just starting to push himself to his feet. Fargo could have sunk a swift kick into his ribs without any trouble. He held back, though, unwilling to kick a man who was still down.

He hoped that decision wouldn't come back to haunt him.

"Get him, Flynn! Smash his head in!" The shouts of encouragement came from Pearsoll's friends as Pearsoll shoved back onto his feet, shaking his head like a bull. He cursed again and looped a roundhouse punch at Fargo's head. Fargo stepped inside and slammed a left and then a right to Pearsoll's guts. Neither blow traveled very far, but they packed all the muscular power of Fargo's body.

Pearsoll rocked back, his ruddy face turning a little pale under its sunburn. He swung wildly again. Fargo ducked to the side, avoiding the punch. He slashed the side of his stiffened hand against the point where Pearsoll's right shoulder met his neck. Pearsoll gasped and staggered, and from the way he held his right arm, Fargo knew that his blow had numbed it.

Pearsoll still had his left, though, and as he swung it in an uppercut, he summoned enough speed so that Fargo wasn't able to get completely out of the way. The fist clipped him on the jaw. Pearsoll was so strong that even the glancing blow was enough to knock Fargo back against the desk.

Fargo slapped a palm down on top of the desk to catch his balance. Roaring again, Pearsoll bored in at him. Pearsoll lifted a kick that splintered the front panel of the desk as Fargo jerked aside from it. That put him within reach of Pearsoll's questing left hand, though. The long, spatulate fingers gripped Fargo's neck.

He knew he was in a bad fix as soon as Pearsoll's hand wrapped around his throat. Pearsoll was strong enough to crush his windpipe, to choke the very life out of him. Fargo reared back on the desk as far as he could. Pearsoll stayed right with him, tightening his hold. As Fargo sprawled on top of the desk, he drew his legs up between them, planted his heels against Pearsoll's chest, and then straightened out like a steel spring uncoiling. Pearsoll's grip on Fargo's throat was torn free, and Pearsoll flew backward through the air, totally out of control.

He slammed into one of the partitions, crashed completely through it, and landed in a tub of filthy water. Fargo bounded after him. By the time he reached the tub, Pearsoll was trying to struggle up out of the water. Fargo put his left hand on top of Pearsoll's head and shoved him under again, holding him there. Pearsoll thrashed around some but was too stunned to overcome being held under the surface.

His friends, who had been whooping and hollering all through the fight, now watched in a stunned silence. Suddenly, one of them found his voice and yelped, "He's gonna drown Flynn!" The hardcase reached for his gun.

Fargo beat him to it, palming out the Colt and leveling it at Pearsoll's companions. "Hold it!" he snapped. "I'm not going to drown him . . . although it's not a bad idea!"

Pearsoll's struggles were growing weaker now. Fargo tangled his fingers in the man's hair and hauled him up into the air. Pearsoll gasped desperately for breath. Fargo let go of him, straightened, and backed off a couple of steps so that he could cover Pearsoll and the others. Slowly, painfully, Pearsoll pulled himself out of the tub and fell onto the floor beside it.

Water quickly puddled around him as it ran off his sodden clothes.

"Get him up and get him out of here," Fargo told Pearsoll's companions. As a couple of the men came forward and struggled to lift the senseless Pearsoll to his feet, Fargo added, "If he's got any money in his pockets, take five dollars and put it on the desk. That'll help pay for the damages."

"Hell, you oughta be responsible for that, mister!" one of the hardcases said. "You're the one who kicked him through that wall!"

"Just do it," Fargo said.

Muttering, the man delved into one of Flynn's pockets and found a five-dollar gold piece. He threw it onto the desk with a contemptuous look at Fargo, who gave an impassive nod.

"Now get him out of here."

"Mister, you've let yourself in for a world of trouble," one of the men warned Fargo.

"There's not any other kind, is there?" Fargo wore a faint smile now.

He didn't holster his gun until all the other men were gone. As he slid the Colt back into leather, the owner of the place poked his head around the corner of the open door. "You're still alive!" he exclaimed, sounding surprised.

"Why wouldn't I be?"

The man stepped tentatively inside. "Well, when Pearsoll came in, I just figured . . ."

"Flynn Pearsoll may have all of Gila City treed," Fargo snapped, "but I don't live here."

"Yeah, but we do," Giddings said. He scrubbed a weary hand over his face and sighed as he looked at the wrecked partition and the damaged desk. "We do."

Fargo scowled as he went back to the stall where he had left the rest of his gear. He finished dressing and came out. Another five-dollar gold piece rang on

19

the desk as Fargo added it to the one that had come from Pearsoll's pocket.

"Pearsoll's grudge is against me, not anybody else," he said. "If he wants me, I'll be around town for a while tomorrow before I ride on."

Giddings paused in sweeping up debris. "Oh, he'll want to see you again, I reckon. But next time, there's liable to be gun smoke in the air."

Fargo returned to the hotel, keeping his eyes open for an ambush as he walked along the street. No one bothered him, though, and when he reached the hotel he went straight upstairs to his room, peeled his clothes off, and fell into bed. He had a few aches and pains from the tussle with Pearsoll, but nothing that kept him from falling asleep almost as soon as his head hit the pillow.

He awoke early in the morning, as was his habit, and got up to stretch the stiffness out of his muscles. When he was dressed, he went to the stable behind the hotel to check on the Ovaro. The big black-and-white stallion was glad to see Fargo, tossing his head and snorting as if trying to tell his master that it was time for them to get back on the trail.

"Not just yet, big fella," Fargo said with a smile as he patted the stallion on the shoulder.

With his horse taken care of, he turned his attention to his own needs. His belly was empty. He walked up the alley beside the hotel and down the street toward Chinese Johnny's place. Quite a few people were already up and around in Gila City, but Fargo didn't see any sign of Flynn Pearsoll or the other hardcases. Pearsoll was probably lying in some whore's crib, trying to recover from the beating he had received or still sleeping off all the whiskey he'd guzzled. Either way, Fargo didn't think Pearsoll represented an immediate threat.

An old wagon with a team of mules hitched to it stood in front of the hash house. Supplies were piled in the back under loosely-tied canvas. Fargo wondered if the wagon belonged to Bert Olmsted and his grand-daughters. When he went inside, he saw that the guess was right. Olmsted, Glory, and Vangie sat at the counter eating breakfast and drinking coffee. A couple of the other stools were occupied by residents of Gila City.

When Johnny saw Fargo he raised a hand in greeting. That made Olmsted and the two young women glance around. Glory and Vangie greeted Fargo with smiles. Olmsted just grunted, looking as hungover as a toad.

"Hello, Skye," Vangie said.

"We were hoping we'd see you again," Glory added.

There was an empty stool beside Glory. Fargo took it, noting her smile and Vangie's frown as he did so. Clearly, there was a lot of competitive spirit between these beautiful cousins. Under other circumstances, that might lead to some interesting developments, but as it was, Fargo figured they wouldn't be around the settlement long enough for that, and neither would he.

"That your wagon parked outside?" he asked as he nodded at Johnny, who held up the coffeepot with an inquisitive look.

"That's right," Glory said.

Johnny put a cup in front of Fargo and filled it. "You want hotcakes and bacon?" he asked.

"Sounds mighty good," Fargo said. To Glory, he said, "It looks like you're about ready to pull out."

"Yes, we've got a ways to go. It'll take most of the day to get back to our diggings."

"Where would that be?"

"North of here a ways, in a canyon east of the Colorado."

"Finding any color?"

Before Glory could answer, Olmsted cleared his throat meaningfully. "Not to speak of," he said.

Fargo doubted that. From Olmsted's reaction, Fargo

thought there was a good chance the old man and his granddaughters had struck gold, and old habits were making Olmsted cautious, even though Fargo had helped him out the night before. Of course, the strike might not amount to much. Most didn't. But some did, and those were the ones that made wealthy men out of their discoverers, even dried-up old prospectors like Olmsted.

"Well, I wish you luck," Fargo said. Johnny put a plate of food in front of him, and he dug in.

The bacon was cooked a little too much, and the hotcakes could have stood a little more cooking, but all in all, breakfast was better than supper had been the night before. And the coffee was still mighty good. As Fargo ate, he became aware that Glory's knee had moved over and was pressing warmly against his. He enjoyed the contact and was willing to bet that she was warm like that all over.

Vangie stood up, walked behind her grandfather and cousin, and put a hand on Fargo's shoulder. "If you wanted to come up and pay us a visit at the diggings, I'm sure it would be fine," she said.

The offer was appealing. If Fargo hadn't had anywhere else to go, he might have taken her up on it. But he had started out for California, and he was determined to get there.

"Sorry," he said, and meant it. "I've got to be riding on west."

"Are you sure?" Glory asked. She sounded disappointed.

"Yeah, but if I ever get through these parts again, I'll be sure to look you up."

"You do that," Vangie said, squeezing his shoulder. Glory's knee rubbed against his.

Fargo downed a healthy slug of the coffee and steeled his resolve. The invitation was tempting indeed.

A few minutes later, Olmsted and the two young women left the hash house after Glory had paid Johnny for their meals. When they were gone, Johnny topped off Fargo's cup of coffee and said, "Not many men would say no to those two."

Fargo smiled. "Maybe I'm just a damned fool."

"No, but I think you not forget them. Some cold, lonely night you remember Miss Vangie and Miss Glory, and you think about what might have been."

"Bet a hat on that," Fargo said.

To tell the truth, though, he wasn't one to dwell on the past or harbor regrets. He believed there were too many good things in the future for him to waste time like that.

He finished his coffee, paid Johnny for the breakfast, and stepped outside, stretching again as he did so. He planned to pick up a few supplies, saddle the Ovaro, and hit the trail to the West.

As that thought crossed his mind, he glanced instinctively in that direction, and as he did so he spotted the wagon topping a small rise just outside of town. Fargo watched it go with a smile on his face, but a moment later that smile was replaced by a slight frown as he saw several riders take the western trail as well. One of them, who bulked large in the saddle, looked familiar even at this distance, with his back to Fargo.

Flynn Pearsoll was the only man he'd seen in Gila City who was that big.

Fargo stood there for a moment, his frown deepening. He remembered Glory telling him that their diggings were north of Gila City, in a canyon east of the Colorado River. The Gila River and the Colorado merged a couple of miles west of the settlement. Chances were the old man and his granddaughters would turn north there and follow the trail that paralleled the Colorado. But there was also a ferry, and the westbound trail continued on the other side of the river. Just because Pearsoll and a few of his friends were heading in that direction out of town didn't mean they were following Olmsted, Glory, and Vangie.

But it didn't mean they weren't, either.

Fargo wasn't one to spend a lot of time pondering a decision. His keen mind was able to boil a situation down to its basics in a hurry, and when he saw the right course to follow, he acted on it without delay. Now he walked quickly to the stable behind the hotel and got the stallion ready to ride.

He still had enough food and ammunition to last him for several days, so it wasn't absolutely necessary that he replenish his supplies here in Gila City. Nor did he have to be in San Francisco by any particular time. So a detour to the north wasn't going to be any problem, Fargo told himself as he swung into the saddle and sent the Ovaro jogging out of the stable. He turned west and took the same trail the wagon and the riders had used.

Fargo wouldn't have been surprised if Pearsoll had braced him this morning and forced a showdown. But from the looks of it, Pearsoll might have diverted his anger and his desire for vengeance back onto Bert Olmsted. That was the assumption Fargo was going to go on until it was proved otherwise. If that turned out to be the case, Fargo intended to stop Pearsoll before Olmsted, Glory, or Vangie could be hurt.

By the time Fargo reached the top of the rise, the wagon and its followers were out of sight. He rode on to the river crossing. The large, flat-bottomed ferry was tied on the eastern side of the Colorado, with its operators lounging on the bank smoking pipes.

"Carried anybody across in the last little while?" Fargo asked the men.

One of them shook his head. "Nope, been a slow mornin' so far, ain't had a single customer. Only folks who've come along took the trail north along the river."

"A wagon with an old man and two young women on it, followed a few minutes later by several men on horseback?"

"Say, that's right, mister." The man frowned. "There ain't some kind of trouble goin' on, is there?"

"I don't know," Fargo said, "but I intend to find out."

He pointed the stallion north and heeled the horse into a fast lope.

The trail was narrow, barely wide enough for an old spring wagon like Olmsted's or a couple of men on horseback riding abreast. Fargo's eyes searched the ground and saw the marks left by the iron-rimmed wheels. The hoofprints of four riders lay atop the wheel marks. Even if the man at the ferry hadn't told him about the riders following the wagon, Fargo would have known. The signs were plain as day to the Trailsman.

He pushed the stallion to a little faster pace. He wanted to catch up to Pearsoll before the big redhead and his companions had a chance to attack the wagon. Fargo didn't know how patient Pearsoll would be; chances were, he would wait until they had put a good distance between themselves and Gila City before risking a murderous ambush, but Fargo couldn't know that for sure. He didn't want to risk the lives of his newfound friends.

After he had gone a couple of miles north, however, he spotted something odd that made him rein to a halt and frown at the marks on the ground. The trail left by Pearsoll and his partners veered off to the right, back to the east. Maybe they weren't following the wagon after all.

Or maybe they were just circling around so that they could get ahead of the vehicle and bushwhack Olmsted and his granddaughters.

That possibility made Fargo prod the Ovaro into a gallop.

The river twisted and turned, and so did the trail that followed it. A few minutes later, Fargo caught sight of the wagon around a bend, but then it disappeared again as the trail took another turn. While it was out of sight, Fargo heard the sudden crackle of gunfire.

He leaned forward in the saddle, urging the stallion on to even greater speed. The big black-and-white horse stretched out, eating up the ground in massive, lunging strides. One-handed, Fargo drew the Henry rifle from its sheath, then grasped it in both hands along with the reins and worked the weapon's lever, throwing a cartridge into the chamber.

He rounded another bend. The trail dipped down close to the river, and to the right loomed a sharp-edged, copper-colored ridge. Men ran along that ridge, firing down at the careening wagon below. Olmsted hunched forward on the driver's seat, yelling encouragement to his team of mules and slashing their rumps with the trailing end of the reins. Glory and Vangie had retreated into the rear of the wagon, where they crouched among the supplies and returned the fire of the ambushers.

Fargo saw to his surprise that the bushwhackers weren't Flynn Pearsoll and his friends. Instead, the men attacking the wagon wore breechcloths, high leather moccasins, colorful shirts, and bright headbands that bound their long black hair.

Apaches.

Fargo had tangled with these fierce warriors before and knew them to be some of the finest fighting men in the world. Equally at home in mountains or desert, able to run at a fast pace all day without tiring, capable of surviving on less food and water than seemed humanly possible, the Apaches possessed both great courage and great cruelty, though they didn't see it as such. To the Apaches, all of life was a test, an ordeal to be endured. The ability to tolerate hardship in all its forms, without crying out or surrendering, was the only true measure of a man.

So they neither expected mercy nor gave it. If they

stopped the wagon, it would mean slow death for Olmsted and degradation for the women.

Fargo brought the Henry to his shoulder and squeezed off three rounds, firing as fast as he could work the lever. He placed the bullets at the feet of the Apaches. The band was a small one, only five or six warriors, and when Fargo's shots kicked up dust at their feet, they wheeled around and shouted their anger. Flame belched from the muzzles of their rifles as they turned their fire on him.

.Fargo left the saddle in a dive. Landing agilely, he rolled over and came up in a crouch. A quick spring took him behind a good-sized rock that perched beside the trail. He gave a shrill whistle, and the signal caused the Ovaro to whirl and dash back up the trail, out of the line of fire. Fargo knelt, sighted over the rock, and triggered two more shots at the Apaches as they charged him. This time he wasn't aiming to spook them. One of his bullets clipped the arm of a warrior. The other came close enough to an Apache's ear to send the man diving for cover.

More shots blasted from the trail. Fargo glanced in that direction and saw to his surprise that the wagon had stopped. Olmsted crouched on the seat, firing up at the Apaches with an old single-shot rifle. Glory and Vangie had leaped down from the wagon and were working their way back along the trail, firing their rifles as they came, peppering the Apaches with slugs from below.

Though they still outnumbered their intended victims, the odds were closer to even now, and the Apaches suddenly broke off their attack. They dashed back to the east, into a wasteland of gullies and sandstone spires. Fargo sent a couple of slugs after them to hurry them on their way. After a few moments, he heard the abrupt rattle of hoofbeats. The Apaches had left horses back in one of those arroyos, and now they fled on the mounts.

They wouldn't forget, though. They would hang on to their grudge at being forced to flee, adding even more resentment to the hatred they felt for the whites they considered invaders of this harsh land.

Fargo waited until he was sure they were gone before he stood up from behind the rock. He saw that Vangie and Glory were only about fifty yards away now. The young women waved their rifles over their heads in greeting. Beyond them, Olmsted was working to turn the wagon and team around on the narrow trail. When he got it done, he drove toward his granddaughters and Fargo.

"My God, Skye, you saved our lives!" Vangie said as they walked up to him.

"Not any more than you helped save my bacon when those Apaches turned around and came after me," Fargo told them with a grin.

"We thought we were goners!" Glory exclaimed. "We never expected to see you again."

"I thought you were headed for California," Vangie said.

Fargo's grin stretched wider. "Sometimes plans get changed."

"Well, I'm glad yours got changed this time," Glory said. "Otherwise those Apaches would've got us for sure!"

The wagon rattled to a stop. "Good morning again, Mr. Fargo," Olmsted said. All the signs of his hangover were gone. Nothing like an Indian attack to clear the cobwebs from a fella's brain, Fargo thought. "What brings you out here?"

Fargo didn't pull any punches. "I saw Flynn Pearsoll and some of his friends follow you out of Gila City. I thought they might intend to bushwhack you, so I came along to give you a hand."

Olmsted's eyes widened. "Pearsoll? We haven't seen any sign of him since leaving town, have we, girls?"

Glory said, "We didn't see anybody until those 'paches jumped us."

"Pearsoll and the others headed off to the east a ways back," Fargo explained. "Maybe they weren't after you at all, or maybe they're still planning to get up to some mischief. Either way, I thought I'd ride with you back to your camp."

Olmsted scraped a hand over the tuft of beard on his chin. "It ain't that I want to seem ungrateful, or inhospitable . . ."

"Oh, stop it, Gramps," Vangie said. She turned to Fargo and went on, "He's just worried because he thinks we might be on to a good strike, and he doesn't want anybody else getting wind of it yet."

"You don't have to worry about me," Fargo assured the old-timer. "I'm not a prospector, and I've had chances to jump claims before now if I'd wanted to. I just want to see that Pearsoll doesn't cause any trouble for you."

"Well, that's mighty nice of you, I reckon," Olmsted allowed. He thought a second longer and then nodded. "Come ahead, then, and welcome. We'll be glad for the company, won't we, girls?"

"We sure will," Glory said.

"That's right," Vangie added.

Fargo whistled for the Ovaro. The stallion came trotting up a moment later. "I meant to pick up some supplies in town before I left," Fargo said as he mounted, "but then I saw Pearsoll ride out and didn't take the time to do it."

"Don't worry about that," Vangie said. "We've got plenty. You can stay as long as you want."

Fargo intended to stay until he was sure that Pearsoll didn't intend them any harm. After that . . . well, he would just have to wait and see how things were going, he told himself.

Olmsted turned the wagon again and pointed it north. Glory climbed onto the seat beside him while Vangie found a place for herself in the back. Fargo rode alongside, carefully scanning their surroundings for anything unusual or any sign of trouble.

"I was about halfway expectin' those savages to jump us on the way back," Olmsted commented as he handled the mule team. "To be honest, though, I thought we'd be closer to the diggins before they did."

"You've had trouble with the Apaches before?" Fargo asked.

"This was the first time they've come gunnin' for us, but the local war chief, a feller called Rafaelito, has a bit of a grudge against us."

"More than the usual Apache grudge, you mean?"

"Yes, he claims that the canyon where our diggins are located is sacred ground to his people, that the spirits of his ancestors live there." Olmsted turned his head to look up at Fargo. "Don't know if that's true or not, but I suppose there must be a reason the bloody place is called Skeleton Canyon."

3

Fargo had never heard of Skeleton Canyon and said as much.

"It's just a little place, about a hundred yards wide and perhaps a quarter of a mile long," Olmsted explained. "I must've walked past it a score of times or more without ever goin' up it to check for gold. But one day I did, and I found a spring at the far end that flows out into a little creek. The creek runs barely more than a stone's throw before it goes back underground. But in that stone's throw we found color, didn't we, girls?"

"We found more than color," Glory said. "We found nuggets."

"And there's always more when it rains in the mountains to the northeast," Vangie added.

Fargo nodded in understanding. The rain made the flow of the creek increase, and that carried more gold down from the lode that was located higher in the mountains.

"Have you tried to figure out where the creek's coming from?" he asked.

"Haven't got that far," Olmsted said. "We've been takin' enough ore out as it is to keep us busy. One of these days, though, we'll do a bit of explorin' . . . if we can keep our hair, that is."

"If the Apaches think you're trespassing on sacred

ground, I'm surprised they haven't attacked you before now."

"I think they've been afraid to come into the canyon and do it," Glory said. "Rafaelito and some of his warriors came right up to the mouth of it one day and called us. We went out to talk to him."

Fargo frowned. "And he didn't try to kill you then?"

"He swore he wouldn't hurt us. He just wanted to ask us to leave the canyon." Glory shrugged. "He speaks a little English, and Vangie and I speak a little Spanish, so we were able to communicate."

Olmsted sniffed. "What you girls speak is American. It ain't the Queen's English, that's certain."

Vangie laughed. "You sound like an American most of the time yourself, Gramps."

"Don't remind me," Olmsted said with a wince.

"What about the Apaches?" Fargo prodded. The story so far struck him as strange. It wasn't like Apaches to parley. On the other hand, they were an unpredictable people, and sometimes they did the unexpected. This so-called Skeleton Canyon had to have them pretty spooked if they refused to enter it.

"Rafaelito told us we had to leave," Vangie said. "He claimed the canyon is haunted by powerful spirits, the spirits of the Old Ones."

"The Old Ones," Fargo repeated, turning the phrase over in his mind.

"That's right. We supposed he meant the ghosts of the Apaches who used to live around here."

Fargo wasn't sure if that was correct or not, but he let it go for the moment.

Glory picked up the story again. "He said if we didn't get out, the spirits would take vengeance on us. Then he said that if the spirits were unhappy, the Apaches would be unhappy, too, and we took that to mean they would attack us. I thought they might do it then, but they just left instead."

"But you haven't had any real trouble from them until today?"

"That's right," Vangie said. "I guess they've been watching us and waiting until we were out of the canyon so they could jump us."

That made sense to Fargo. If everything they told him was true, the Apaches presented an even greater threat than normal . . . and they were plenty dangerous to start with.

There was also still the potential threat of Flynn Pearsoll. The more Fargo thought about it, the more he knew he had made the right decision by riding after Olmsted and his granddaughters. Surrounded by enemies as they were, they were going to need help to survive in this rugged, semiarid wilderness.

As Glory had indicated that morning, it took most of the day to reach their destination. The river flowed to their left, sometimes through deep canyons, and to their right rose several ranges of mountains and hills. Vegetation was sparse: clumps of grass here and there, an occasional hardy bush, and scrubby pines on the slopes of some of the hills. The region had a certain stark beauty, but overall it looked as harsh and unforgiving as it was.

Late in the day they reached a line of red sandstone cliffs that marched along the eastern horizon, forming an escarpment a hundred feet high. The cliffs were unbroken until they came to a narrow canyon that cut into them like a knife slash. Beyond the canyon the cliffs resumed their solid bulwark for as far as Fargo could see.

"There it is," Olmsted announced. "Skeleton Canyon."

With the sun lowering in the west as it was, the light should have shone all the way up into the canyon. But as the travelers reached the mouth of it, Fargo saw that the sheer stone walls somehow cast shadows, so that the canyon looked less than inviting. Olmsted turned the mules into it without hesitation, though.

The canyon ran mostly straight, but there was one bend in it, and it was a fairly sharp one. That meant the area beyond the bend was even more shadowy. Normally, the air in this corner of Arizona was furnacelike, but here there was a hint of coolness, as if the heat of the baking sun seldom penetrated. When they came around the bend, Fargo saw the little stream and the tents pitched alongside it.

"Home, sweet home," Glory said with a rather humorless laugh.

"It may not look like much," Vangie put in, "but if it makes us rich then it's mighty pretty to me."

"Might as well be Buckingham Palace," Olmsted said. "Not that I'm all that familiar with the palace, mind. My family wasn't royalty, no sirree bob."

"Gramps was a remittance man," Glory said.

Fargo nodded. "Known a few of them in my time. Most were good men who just had the bad luck to be born second."

"Good luck as far as I'm concerned," Olmsted said. "What kind of a life would that be, sittin' around drawin' rooms sippin' tea all day? Butlers to wait on you hand and foot, and a fancy carriage and driver to take you wherever you want to go. I thank the Good Lord I don't have to live like that."

Fargo thought there was a certain note of wistfulness in Olmsted's voice, though. He might have enjoyed trying that life, at least for a little while.

But Fargo knew what the Englishman meant. Once a man got used to living on the frontier, he didn't want to spend his days anywhere else. Life out here could be hard and dangerous, but it was also free.

Olmsted brought the wagon to a halt beside the tents and hopped down with a spryness that belied his age. Glory and Vangie followed him. Fargo swung down from the saddle, still looking around. The canyon would be easy to defend, he thought, but under certain circumstances it could also serve as a death-trap.

"Is there any other way in and out?" he asked.

"Not really," Olmsted said. "There's a place or two where you might be able to climb out, but a man'd have to be half mountain goat to manage it."

A dark smudge on one of the walls caught Fargo's eye. He pointed and said, "What's that?"

"A cave, I think. Never been up there to see. No reason to."

In the fading light, Fargo's eyes picked out a narrow ledge that led to the mouth of the cave. A man could probably negotiate that ledge if he had to, but it would be a harrowing climb and one misstep would send him plummeting to the ground far below. And as far as he could tell, the ledge didn't continue on beyond the cave mouth, which meant there was even less reason to climb up there. It might have been different if the ledge had ascended all the way to the top of the canyon.

Glory and Vangie started unloading the supplies and carrying them into the tents. Fargo pitched in to help. There were three tents, one for the old man and one for each of his granddaughters.

"I hope you don't mind sleeping in the open," Glory commented.

Fargo chuckled. "I've spent a lot of my life doing just that," he said. "If it rains, I'll get under the wagon."

Of course, if it rained very much, they would all want to get out of the canyon to avoid the chance of a flash flood. It didn't rain very often in these parts, but when it did, the downpour was sometimes a real gully washer.

Fargo kept an eye on the canyon walls. Glory noticed what he was doing and said, "You think somebody's going to try to pick us off from up there?"

"It's a good spot for it," Fargo said. "Rafaelito's band of Apaches could come back, and Pearsoll and his bunch are still out there somewhere."

"You talk like we should just give up and leave because it's dangerous, Skye," Vangie said.

"Nope. That's your decision. If you haven't been standing guard at night, though, I reckon it'd be a good idea to start. I'll take one of the watches, too."

They agreed with the idea. As the last of the daylight faded away, Olmsted kindled a fire and Glory and Vangie got busy preparing supper. They had all made do with jerky and hard biscuits for lunch on the trail. Fargo was looking forward to some hot food.

Vangie carved thick slabs off a side of bacon and got them frying in a pan while Glory put beans on to cook in a black iron pot. The beans had been soaking all the way from Gila City. Olmsted lit a pipe and stood nearby with his rifle tucked under his arm. Fargo unhitched the mules and hobbled them on a patch of grass beside the creek. Then he unsaddled the Ovaro and turned him loose. The stallion wouldn't wander off.

One of the cousins had set a coffeepot at the edge of the fire to boil. Soon the delicious aromas of coffee and bacon and beans filled the canyon, and it didn't seem like such an eerie, forbidding place. When the food was ready, Fargo sat down cross-legged on the ground and took the tin plate Vangie gave him. He ate with a hearty appetite.

"What do you think?" Vangie asked after a few minutes.

"Food's better than Chinese Johnny's," Fargo said honestly. The coffee wasn't as good, but he didn't mention that.

Olmsted snorted. "Wouldn't take much to better that Chinaman's cooking. Still, he's not a bad sort for a heathen."

Fargo helped clean up after the meal was finished. He took note of the fact that all three of his companions looked tired. He was somewhat weary himself after a day spent mostly in the saddle, but he knew his reserves of strength were probably greater than theirs. "I'll take the first watch," he volunteered, and he added silently to himself that he would stay up as long as he could so that the others could get a little extra sleep.

"Mighty good of you, Fargo," Olmsted muttered. "Believe I'll go turn in." He headed for one of the tents.

"Good night, Skye," Glory said as she came over to him. "If you need me, I'll be in that tent right over there." She pointed to make sure he knew which one she was talking about.

"And that's my tent," Vangie said as she came up on Fargo's other side. She pointed, too. "That one."

Fargo tried not to grin. They were being pretty obvious with their invitations . . . not that he intended to take either one of them up on it. No matter how pretty Glory and Vangie were, he wouldn't feel right about romping with either cousin while the other one was so close by, not to mention their grandfather.

Besides, he didn't need that distraction while he was standing guard. He still wasn't convinced there wouldn't be trouble of some sort tonight.

Reluctantly, the two young women left him alone and went into their tents. Fargo sat down next to the wagon and propped his back against a wheel, holding the Henry across his knees. He planned to get up and take a stroll around the camp on a fairly regular basis. In the meantime, he avoided looking into the campfire. Even though the flames were dying down, they still gave off enough light to ruin a man's night vision if he looked at them long enough.

A coyote howled in the distance, and Fargo heard another faint sound that might have been a mountain lion crying out on one of the peaks to the east. An owl hooted. Down in Texas, the Comanches liked to hoot like that when they were closing in on somebody they were going to attack. They used the sounds as signals. Apaches did things like that, too, but Fargo judged that what he heard was the real thing. A slight scraping noise was a snake slithering over sand and rock. The creek added a quiet bubbling to the night sounds.

Movement caught Fargo's eye as he glanced around the camp. The entrance flap on Vangie's tent twitched aside. She crawled out.

If Fargo had made a bet with himself on which of the cousins snuck out of her tent and came to see him tonight, he would have picked Vangie. Glory, for all the bold looks she had given him, seemed just a bit more reserved and less likely to act on impulse. Vangie, though, wanted what she wanted when she wanted it.

Fargo suspected that tonight she wanted him.

She came over to him, walking quietly. She had taken off her boots but still wore her denim trousers and mannish shirt. Several of the shirt's buttons were now open, however, and it was spread far enough apart so that he could see the dark cleft between her full breasts, even in the faint starlight. She sank to the ground and sat cross-legged beside him.

"I couldn't sleep," she whispered. "Is it all right if I sit here with you for a while, Skye?"

"Sure," he said, keeping his own voice quiet, too. "Glory may not think so if she finds out about it, though."

"I don't care what Glory thinks. She's not my boss."

"No, you're your own boss, aren't you?" Fargo said.

Vangie grinned up at him. "Damn straight. I do what I want, and right now I want to be with you, Skye."

She leaned closer to him. He felt the warm pressure of her breast against his arm. All he had to do was turn a little to slip his hand into her shirt and fill his palm with the soft weight of her other breast. His thumb found her hard nipple and stroked it. Vangie sighed in pleasure.

Fargo was going to disappoint her, though. "This isn't a good idea," he said.

She put her hands over his and pressed it harder against her breast. "Why not?" she asked breathlessly.

"We're liable to wake the others—"

"I don't care!" Vangie hissed.

"I do," Fargo said. "Besides, I'm supposed to be standing guard, and I can't do a very good job of it if I'm thinking about fooling around with you instead."

"Then why . . ." She had to take a deep breath before she could go on. "Why did you start doing what you're doing? Skye, if you knew how much I want you . . ." She reached over to his lap and found the hard shaft jutting up against the front of his trousers. "And I can tell you want me! You can't tease me like this!"

"It's not a tease," Fargo said. "It's a promise. When the time is right, we'll do whatever you want."

She laughed softly. "As often as I want to do it?"

"As often as you want to do it," Fargo vowed. To seal the bargain, he brought his mouth down on hers in a hot, hungry kiss. Her lips parted, inviting his tongue to spear into the warm, wet cavern and slide deliciously around her tongue.

The kiss filled Fargo with pleasurable sensations, but it didn't dull his senses or his instincts. Only a few seconds had gone by before he knew that something was wrong.

He lifted his head, breaking the kiss. Vangie made a little sound of disappointment in her throat. She must have felt the way Fargo tensed, though, because she whispered, "What's wrong?"

"Don't know," Fargo said, turning his head to look around. "Just feels like something's not the way it's supposed to be . . ."

His jaw tightened as he looked up at the wall of the canyon where the cave mouth was located. A yellow glow, so faint as to be almost invisible, came from the cave.

Fargo touched Vangie's arm and then pointed. She

caught her breath sharply as she looked and saw the glow, too. "What in the world . . . ?"

"None of you have ever been up there?" Fargo asked.

"I don't think so. I know I never have been. How could anybody be in there now? Nobody could have gotten past us and gone up that ledge!"

"Maybe they came in from the other way," Fargo said.

He should have thought of that earlier, he told himself. A cave like that could have another entrance up above, on top of the cliffs. It would be a back door into the canyon, another way in and out. It might even be man-made, by those Old Ones the Apache war chief Rafaelito had mentioned.

"What are we going to do?" Vangie asked.

"You go wake up Glory and your grandfather and let them know something's going on." Fargo's hands tightened on the rifle. "I'm going to go have a look up there."

She clutched at his arm. "Skye, no! If anything happens to you, I . . . I don't know what we'd do."

"If anything comes at me on that narrow ledge, I won't have any trouble picking it off," Fargo assured her. He uncoiled from the ground, and Vangie came with him. He swatted her on the rump. "Go do what I told you."

She muttered a curse, and he knew she didn't like being bossed around. But she hurried toward the tents anyway, running lightly over the sandy ground of the canyon floor.

Fargo stalked toward the spot where the ledge began, keeping an eye on the cave mouth as he did so. Over by the stream, the mules shifted around uneasily, and the Ovaro let out a quiet whinny. The big stallion sensed that something odd was going on, too.

Fargo reached the bottom of the ledge. It didn't come quite all the way to the ground, ending about two feet above the canyon floor. Fargo made the step up, holding the Henry in his right hand while he used his left to steady himself against the rock wall. The climb was fairly steep. The slope was irregular, but Fargo figured it averaged somewhere between twenty and thirty degrees. The ledge was anywhere from a foot and a half to two feet wide.

He had excellent balance and wasn't afraid of heights, but that climb up the side of the canyon wall in nearly total darkness was enough to draw his nerves taut. He kept his left hand pressed against the wall. Behind him, he heard a murmur of low-pitched voices that told him Vangie had roused Olmsted and Glory from sleep.

Fargo could have waited on the ground to see what, if anything, emerged from the cave. That probably would have been a wiser course of action, he told himself as he inched his way up the ledge. At the very least he should have waited until morning to explore the cave.

But something seemed to draw him on . . . a curiosity to know what was up there, to be sure, but he sensed it was more than that. He remembered the story of how, back in the old days of the Greeks and suchlike, some women called Sirens used to sit on a rocky island and sing a song that was so sweet and haunting, any sailors who heard it had no choice but to bring their boats closer and closer until finally the vessels were torn to bits by the rocks and the waves. That was sort of the way Fargo felt now, compelled to climb higher and higher toward that faint, mocking light that filled the mouth of the cave . . .

Then he heard the music drifting from the cave as well, low and erratic, but still powerful. He stopped where he was on the ledge, his eyes widening and his lips drawing back from his teeth in a grimace. The sounds seemed to take physical hold of him and try to draw him onward, but now he realized he never should have come up here. He tried to pull back, struggling against whatever mysterious power had him

41

in its grip. Despite the coolness of the night, beads of sweat popped out on his forehead.

Then suddenly, as the wind sprang up harder and chilled the sweat on his face, he realized what he was hearing and felt its power over him break. It was the wind, he thought, just the wind blowing through the cave. There had to be an opening on the other end, whether it was large enough for a man or not, and when the wind blew through the passage it created those eerie sounds. That was all it was, Fargo told himself.

But it wasn't the wind causing the light inside the cave. Now that he had come this far, he was still determined to investigate that.

He might have, too, if he hadn't heard something else that caught his attention. Somewhere out there in the night, hoofbeats were swiftly approaching the canyon.

Despite th
ped out on h
44—I

4

Fargo started back down the ledge as the hoofbeats grew louder. They echoed from the sandstone walls as the riders entered the canyon. Fargo looked down at the camp and saw that Olmsted and the two young women had heard the sounds, too, and had retreated behind the wagon. Starlight glittered on the barrels of their rifles.

Apaches sometimes attacked at night, though that wasn't their usual pattern. They also preferred to slip up on an enemy on foot until they could leap out from cover and attack at close range. Seldom did they fight on horseback. Though Fargo couldn't rule it out, he didn't think the riders coming up the canyon were Apaches.

Pearsoll's bunch? he asked himself. It was possible.

He moved quickly as he tried to get back to the canyon floor, but he could only go so fast on the ledge, where a single slip could be fatal. Not only that, but the knowledge that he had turned his back on the cave mouth gnawed at his brain. If someone—or something—came out of there now, he might not be able to turn around in time to defend himself, even if he was aware of the threat.

Riders swept around the bend in the canyon while Fargo was still a good thirty feet above the ground. He froze where he was, knowing that if he remained motionless, the newcomers might not notice him on the shadowy ledge. His buckskins would blend in with the canyon wall, at least to a certain extent.

And if any shooting broke out, he had a good vantage point from which to join the fray, although once an enemy spotted him, he would be a sitting duck. There was no cover at all on the ledge.

Three riders reined in about thirty feet from the camp. Men and horses bulked blackly against the lighter-colored sandy floor of the canyon. One of the men edged his mount a little ahead of the others and called out, "You there, Olmsted?"

Obviously, at least one of these men wasn't a stranger to the old prospector, but that didn't mean they were friends. There was a wary edge in Olmsted's voice as he replied, "We're here. What do you want, Mahaffey?"

"Jessel said he thought he saw your wagon earlier today," the man called Mahaffey replied. "Just thought we'd ride over and say hello."

"Thought you'd ride over and see if we'd been to the assay office in Gila City, that's what you mean," Olmsted shot back. The dislike and suspicion in his voice were plain to hear.

At first, Mahaffey had tried to sound friendly, even though his phony sincerity wouldn't fool anybody, Fargo thought. Now he abandoned the effort as he snapped, "You've got no call to talk like that, Olmsted. What did we ever do to you?"

"Nothin' but hang around like a bunch of bloody vultures and wait to take over my claim! I'm surprised we didn't find you here makin' yourself at home when we got back."

"I'm a law-abiding man," Mahaffey said. "This is your claim, duly registered in Gila City. If you don't want to be friends with your neighbors, that's your own damned business! Come on, boys!" He wheeled his horse, ready to ride away. But he couldn't resist one last, over-the-shoulder gibe. "But when Rafaelito comes to lift your hair, don't look to us for help!"

"I wouldn't look to you for nothin'!" Olmsted shouted after him as the three men rode off.

Fargo kept a close eye on them just in case they decided to double back and start shooting. They rode around the bend and kept going, the hoofbeats fading as they left the canyon.

Then and only then did Fargo look back up at the cave behind him.

The entrance was dark now, nothing but a black smudge on the canyon wall. Whatever had been causing the light in there was gone.

Fargo descended the rest of the way to the canyon floor. By the time he got there, Olmsted, Glory, and Vangie had come out from behind the wagon and were waiting for him.

"Did you see them?" Olmsted asked.

"I saw them. Who were they?"

"Mahaffey, Jessel, and Luman. A bunch of damned claim jumpers, if you ask me."

"You've had trouble with them?"

"Not really," Glory said. "They just show up from time to time and act like they're trying to find out if we've struck gold yet. They say they're prospectors, too, but I've never seen any evidence that they actually work at it."

"Neither have I," Vangie added.

Fargo nodded. Every time men began prospecting for gold or silver or other precious minerals, individuals such as Glory had just described showed up as well, scavengers who were content to hang around while someone else did all the work and then move in and try to take advantage of it. Sometimes a whole gang of them would wipe out the honest miners and get rich on their victim's labor. Fargo had faced their likes before, and he was sure he would again.

"They'll never get their filthy hands on any gold that I find," Olmsted vowed. "I'll fight them or anybody else who tries to take it away from me."

"Maybe you'd better find the mother lode before

you get your dander up so much, Gramps," Glory said.

"That's right," Vangie said. "You don't need to work yourself up into a state."

"I ain't workin' myself up into a state," Olmsted grumbled. He turned back to Fargo. "Did you find out what was up there in that cave?"

Fargo shook his head. "Never got there. I heard the riders coming and turned back. But whatever it is must be gone now. There's no more light coming from the cave."

"I thought I heard some sort of music," Glory said tentatively, as if the others might think she was crazy.

Fargo put that notion to rest in a hurry. "You heard something, all right—the wind blowing through that cave. Water carves holes through this sandstone, and when the wind blows just right, it's like wind passing through the pipes of an organ. It makes noises that sound like music, even though they're really not."

"You're right!" Glory exclaimed. "A pipe organ is exactly what it sounded like."

Fargo didn't mention that for a second he had wondered if the sounds were somehow supernatural in origin, like the songs of those old Sirens back in Greece. Even a practical, hardheaded hombre like the Trailsman was entitled to a flight of fancy every once in a while.

The rest of the night passed quietly. Olmsted and his granddaughters crawled back into their tents and went to sleep. Fargo stood watch for several hours, dividing his attention among the canyon rims, the bend, and the mouth of the cave. He didn't see anything suspicious anywhere. Along toward dawn, he finally got a few hours of sleep while the others each stood a short turn on guard duty.

The smell of coffee woke him. Vangie had taken the final shift and had started breakfast as the sun rose over the mountains to the east. The canyon was

46

still in shadow, as it would be most of the day except for a short time when the sun was directly overhead.

Fargo unrolled from his blankets, then stood up and stretched the kinks out of his muscles. Vangie smiled up at him from the campfire, where she was slicing bacon into a pan.

"I guess you were right last night, Skye," she said quietly. "Even if we had started anything, we would have been interrupted . . . and I'm not sure I could have stood that."

Fargo laughed. "There'll be another time."

"Damn right there will. And I'm going to hold you to your promise."

"I'll be waiting," Fargo told her with a grin.

He felt genuine liking for both of the cousins. They were plainspoken and courageous, ready to grab up a rifle and go to shooting any time trouble broke out, and they certainly weren't blushing innocents. Frontier women had to develop harder edges than their gentler sisters back east. And yet Vangie and Glory both managed to remain beautiful and feminine despite their rugged surroundings.

"Coffee should be ready," Vangie said.

Fargo knelt by the fire and used a thick piece of leather as a potholder. He poured himself a cup of the steaming black brew and sipped it appreciatively.

"If you don't mind my asking, Skye, how long do you intend to stay with us?"

"Worn out my welcome already, have I?" Fargo said, still grinning.

"Not hardly! I just know you said you were on your way to California."

"I'll get there when I get there," Fargo said. "I'm not worried about it. I want to give you a hand if I can. It looks to me like you and your cousin and your grandfather have trouble coming at you from at least three different directions."

"The Apaches, Pearsoll and his friends, and those would-be claim jumpers," Vangie said.

Fargo nodded. "That's right. If the Apaches believe this is sacred ground, they won't let you stay here forever. Sooner or later they'll try to drive you out."

"Or sooner or later we'll have to leave for supplies again, and they'll jump us like they did yesterday."

"More than likely," Fargo agreed. "With Pearsoll, you can't be sure what he'll do. A man like that will want to settle the score . . . but at the same time he's capable of getting tired of holding a grudge and moving on. He's like a coiled rattler: you don't know if he's going to strike or just make some racket."

Vangie shivered. "I hate snakes."

Fargo smiled and went on, "Then you've got Mahaffey and his pards. I reckon your grandfather's kept it pretty quiet about what the three of you have found up here."

"Glory and I took the gold to the assay office yesterday, and we didn't talk to anybody except the man who runs it, Mr. Richmond. Gramps went off to the Pine Tree Saloon, of course, and got drunk, so I don't know what he might have said. He told us he wanted to keep it under his hat, though."

"Don't recall him wearing a hat," Fargo pointed out, "but I didn't hear him say anything about gold while I was around him. In fact, he was trying to cadge a drink off Pearsoll, which is what started the whole ruckus. I think most folks who saw that would figure that he hasn't had any luck out here."

"Then we're probably safe from Mahaffey and his friends for now," Vangie said. "I don't think they'll try to get rid of us until they *know* there's gold here."

"But once they do, your lives may be in danger," Fargo said.

Vangie shrugged. "You're right about that." She didn't seem overly worried.

Fargo sipped the coffee and took a deep breath, relishing the smell of the bacon frying. "I'll stick around for a while, just to see how the hand plays out," he said. "For one thing, I want to take a look at that cave in the daylight."

"That's right, we never did find out if anything was up there last night. That could be yet another danger for us."

Fargo wasn't sure that whatever had caused that mysterious glow represented a threat, but he couldn't discount the possibility, either. He glanced up at the cave mouth. It seemed innocent enough this morning.

The aromas of coffee brewing and food cooking roused Glory and Olmsted as well. They came out of their tents and greeted Fargo and Vangie. After the events of the night before, everyone looked and felt a little sleepy, but breakfast went a long way toward waking them up.

When the meal was finished, Fargo walked toward the ledge. Glory called after him, "You're going back up there?"

"That's right. I want to see what's inside the cave."

Olmsted stood up. "You want me to come with you, lad?"

Fargo shook his head and said, "No, stay down here. That way, just in case there's any trouble, the girls won't be left alone."

Vangie sniffed. "We protect Gramps more than the other way around," she said. Olmsted scratched his head, gave a sheepish grin, and didn't argue the matter.

Fargo left the Henry rifle leaning against a wagon wheel. If he needed a gun, he had the Colt, and it only took one hand to use it. He used his left to steady himself against the canyon wall as he stepped up and started the climb again.

It went quickly this morning, now that Fargo could see where he was going and didn't have to feel his way along. He reckoned the cave mouth was about seventy feet above the canyon floor. As he approached it, he rested his right hand on the butt of the holstered revolver.

There wasn't much wind this morning, so the eerie notes of the night before were no longer playing. Just enough of a breeze blew so that as the ledge leveled out and Fargo reached the entrance, he smelled a faint musty odor wafting toward him. It smelled like dust and death.

That didn't have to mean anything. Some animal could have crawled up in there and died. Fargo sniffed again. No scent of fresh droppings, so likely the cave was unoccupied at the moment. He drew the Colt and stepped into the cave mouth, stooping a little so that he wouldn't hit his head on the roof.

The entrance was wide enough so that Fargo was able to go through it without any trouble. The floor angled up slightly, and once he was inside the roof lifted so that he was able to stand straight again. He paused, listening intently, but heard nothing.

The morning light didn't penetrate very far into the cave. Fargo reached into a pocket with his left hand and brought out a match. He flicked the lucifer to life with his thumbnail, squinting against the sudden glare. As his eyes adjusted, he saw that the cave widened out slightly as it went back into the canyon wall. The roof remained a few inches above the crown of his hat. He walked forward, his footsteps muffled by the thick layer of dust on the floor but still loud enough to echo a little.

He saw some dried-out brush that had probably been dragged into the cave to serve as an animal's nest. Here and there, black smudges showed on the walls, a sign that fires had been built in here a long time ago. Fargo suddenly caught his breath as the flickering light revealed drawings on the walls, etched into the soft sandstone by some sort of tool. He had seen ancient cave drawings and paintings before, mute testaments to the lives of those who had lived hundreds, perhaps thousands, of years earlier. He knew he was looking at the same thing here, messages coming down through time from the people who had originally occupied this place.

He studied the drawings as the match burned down in his fingers. Feeling its heat, he swung away from the walls and turned again toward the rear of the cave.

The flame reached his fingers, and he instinctively shook it out just as its glow showed him the naked skull leering at him from the darkness.

Fargo's breath hissed between his teeth and he took an involuntary step back as the gun in his hand came up. His pulse hammered wildly for a moment inside his head. His brain forced rationality back into his body. Yes, he had seen a skull, he told himself, but whoever it belonged to, the gent couldn't hurt him now. Fargo found another match and lit it.

The skeleton sat against the rear wall of the cave with its bony legs stretched out in front of it. Fargo knelt, holding the match out for a better look. He was no expert on such things, but judging by the size of the skeleton, it must have belonged to a man, and a fairly large one at that. Fargo looked for bullet holes, broken bones, or any other sign of injury. He didn't see any, which meant that the man hadn't crawled in here and died of wounds after a fight. Fargo's eyes narrowed as he saw something else. He moved the match flame closer to the skeleton's right arm.

An iron band encircled the wrist, and it was attached to a chain that lay on the floor of the cave, almost buried in the dust of years. The chain led to the wall against which the skeleton leaned and was fastened there by a pin driven deep into the rock. Fargo picked up the chain—the clinking of the links against each other sounding uncannily loud in the stillness—and tugged hard on it. It didn't budge.

Well, he knew how the fella had died, he told himself. Somebody had chained him up in this cave and left the poor bastard here to starve to death.

Fargo's jaw tightened in anger. He didn't know who

this man had been or what he might have done to bring such a fate down on himself, but it still seemed like a hell of a cruel thing to do to anybody.

The man was long past caring now. Fargo stood up and cast a quick glance around the rest of the cave. There was nothing to see, only stone walls and dust. This makeshift tomb had been undisturbed for a long, long time.

But if that was true, Fargo asked himself, how had there been a light in here last night?

He couldn't answer that. He knew only that there was no rear exit from the cave, only some tiny holes through which the wind blew and produced the strange music he had heard. He dropped the second match and turned toward the entrance. The light from outside outlined it sharply against the dimness of the cave.

Fargo holstered his gun as he stepped out onto the ledge. He looked down and saw Olmsted, Glory, and Vangie waiting for him, their faces turned up as they watched the mouth of the cave. He waved at them to let them know everything was all right and then started back down the ledge.

"What did you find?" Glory asked as he reached the bottom.

"Maybe the reason this place is called Skeleton Canyon," Fargo said. "There's what's left of an hombre up there in the cave."

"Dead, you mean?" Olmsted asked, eyes wide.

Fargo nodded. "Dead as can be, and for a long time, to boot. I'd guess he's been up there at least a hundred years, probably longer."

"One of the Old Ones Rafaelito talked about?" Vangie asked.

"No way of knowing. He seemed like a big fella, but that's all I could tell about him. Well, that and the fact that he'd been chained to the wall."

"Chained!" The exclamation came in unison from all three of them.

"That's right. He was a prisoner of some sort. Probably starved to death, maybe deliberately, or maybe something happened to his keepers. No matter what, I reckon it was a pretty bad way to go."

"Poor devil," Olmsted muttered. He tugged on his beard. "I say, do you think we should bring him down and give him a proper burial?"

"I had the same idea," Fargo said. "I've had to leave a few men for the buzzards in my time, but I never liked it. No matter what that fella did, he ought to be laid to rest decent-like."

"I agree. I've got a chisel we can use to cut the chain."

"What about your prospecting?"

"The gold's been there a long time," Olmsted said. "It can wait a while longer."

Fargo took the chisel and a hammer and a blanket back up to the cave, along with a lantern to give better light as he worked. It didn't take long to break the chain. When he had done that, he paused for a moment to inspect the iron band around the skeleton's right wrist. When he touched it, he felt something etched into the metal and brought the lantern closer so he could see better. He blew dust off the iron and discovered strange symbols carved into it. Maybe they were letters that formed words in a forgotten tongue. Fargo didn't know, because he had never seen anything like them before. With a shake of his head, he lowered the bony arm.

He bundled the skeleton up in the blanket and carried it out of the cave. The burden was an awkward one as Fargo brought it back down the ledge, so he had to be mighty careful. The bones seemed to weigh more than they should have, too, almost as if the living flesh was still on them.

It wasn't easy finding a good burial site in this rocky country, but Olmsted and his granddaughters had located one near the head of the canyon, close to the spot where the spring bubbled up from underground. They had already started digging the grave. Fargo lowered the grisly bundle to the ground and pitched in to help and by midmorning they had the grave ready.

Fargo and Olmsted placed the blanket-wrapped bones in the grave. Glory and Vangie took turns with the shovel, covering it up, while Fargo and the old-timer found some good-sized rocks to stack over it in a sort of cairn.

When they were finished and had mounded the rocks over the grave, Fargo and the girls took their hats off and stood there with Olmsted. "Somebody ought to say something," the old man commented.

"Wouldn't rightly know what," Fargo said. "We don't know how this fella worshipped or what he believed. But I reckon *El Señor Dios* has been watching over him all the time he's been up there in that cave, and it won't be any different now."

"Amen," Glory said quietly, and Vangie echoed, "Amen."

"Well," Olmsted said, "it's back to work, I suppose."

They turned to walk away from the grave, heading back toward camp. Olmsted strode on ahead, but Glory and Vangie dropped back to walk alongside Fargo. "Skye," Vangie said, "we were just wondering . . ."

"What made that light in the cave last night if there was nothing up there but a skeleton?" Fargo finished for her.

"Yes," Glory said.

"I don't know," Fargo said with a shake of his head. "I don't have a blessed idea."

A couple of days passed quietly. Olmsted worked along the edge of the creek, panning out not only gold dust but several small nuggets as well. Glory and Vangie had some diggings started in the canyon wall near the spring, where Olmsted thought they would be most likely to find an actual vein of gold. Fargo worked with them, tirelessly swinging a pickax, gouging chunks of rock from the wall. They had penetrated the upper layer of sandstone and were into the quartz behind it. Fargo had been around enough mining operations in the past so that he felt optimistic about their chances of making a strike. The place had the right look about it.

From time to time he found himself glancing over his shoulder toward the grave, some twenty yards away. It made him uneasy, but he told himself that was foolish. Humans had a natural fear of death, and nothing symbolized death more than the bones left behind when life had departed. But bones couldn't *do* anything. They didn't represent any real threat.

Not like the Apaches.

Fargo was taking a break, late in the afternoon, when he saw the tiny flicker of red on the canyon rim. Without seeming to pay much attention, he watched the place closer, and a few moments later he was rewarded by another brief flash of color. Somebody was up there, and considering how the Apaches liked to use red cloth for their headbands, he thought it was a good bet Rafaelito and his warriors had come back.

Fargo didn't know if the Apaches were there to ambush them or just to keep an eye on the white interlopers. He had brought the Henry rifle with him to the diggings, as was his habit, and left it leaning against the canyon wall. He drifted toward it now, just in case, while Glory swung the pick and Vangie pawed through the pieces of rock that came off the wall, looking for color. As Fargo moved, Vangie glanced over at him, then looked again and said, "What's wrong, Skye?"

"Somebody up on the rim," Fargo said in a low voice. "My guess is it's Apaches, but I don't know that."

Glory lowered the pick. "What should we do?"

"Keep working like there's nothing wrong," Fargo

told her. "If they're just watching us, they'll get tired of it after a while and go away."

"And if they're not?" Vangie asked.

Fargo's answering smile was grim. "Then we'll know that before long, too."

Fargo's prediction was right. They didn't have to wait long. He saw sunlight glint on a rifle barrel, and then a shot blasted out. Down the creek, the bullet splashed into the water near Bert Olmsted. Fargo snatched up the Henry and yelled, "Run!" at the old-timer. "Head for the wagon, girls!" he shouted at Glory and Vangie as he began to blaze away at the rim.

It came back to him, then, what he had thought about this canyon the first time he saw it. He had told himself then that it might turn out to be a death-trap . . .

They were about to put that to the test.

5

Vangie and Glory dashed past Fargo, heading for the wagon. Olmsted was already there. The old-timer threw himself on the ground and crawled under the vehicle. When he came up on the other side, he had his rifle in his hands. He poked the barrel over the wagon bed and searched for a target on the rim.

The Apaches were too clever to reveal themselves carelessly. Fargo triggered five shots as fast as he could work the Henry's lever, peppering the rim with lead. He hoped that would make the warriors duck for cover and give him a chance to reach the wagon, too. He brought the rifle down and broke into a run.

Vangie glanced back over her shoulder at him and screamed, "Skye, look out! Above you!"

Fargo's gaze flicked upward in time to see the large rock plummeting toward him. He left his feet in a dive. The rock whistled down through the space he had occupied an instant earlier and crashed to the canyon floor, embedding itself slightly in the sand. If it had landed on Fargo's head, it would have crushed his skull like an eggshell.

So the Apaches were on this side of the canyon, too, he thought as he rolled over and surged back up. He resumed his dash toward the wagon.

Glory and Vangie had reached it by now and snatched up their rifles. They joined their grandfather in burning powder, twisting back and forth so that they could throw lead at both rims of the canyon. The angle was bad when they aimed at the nearer rim, though, and Fargo didn't think they would be able to do much damage on that side. The Apaches, however, could continue to rain down rocks on top of them.

Fargo dropped into a crouch beside one of the wagon wheels. He brought the Henry to his shoulder, waited a second, and then squeezed off a shot as he saw another flash of color on the far rim. He was rewarded by a yelp of pain. He had scored at least one hit in this battle, he told himself. But that wouldn't be anywhere near enough to drive off the Apaches.

More rocks crashed down, one of them only a few feet from the wagon. Glory and Vangie both flinched and cried out involuntarily. Bullets whined off stone and thudded into the thick planks of the wagon. They were caught between a rock and a hard place, Fargo thought. If they stayed where they were, sooner or later the bullets or the falling boulders would get them.

"Concentrate your fire on the far rim," Fargo barked at Glory and Vangie. "Cover me!"

"What are you going to do?" Glory asked, but the question came too late. Fargo had already crawled under the wagon, come out on the other side, and leaped up to sprint toward the creek.

Bullets from above kicked up dust around his booted feet as he ran. Behind him, rifles cracked and roared as Olmsted and his granddaughters threw a deadly barrage at the far rim. The Apaches had good cover up there, so the storm of lead probably wouldn't do much damage, but at least their firing fell off as they hunkered lower behind the rocks.

The stream was shallow, no more than a foot deep. Fargo splashed across it without slowing down and headed for a small cluster of boulders near the far wall. He threw himself down among the rocks, twisted around, and looked up at the rim above the wagon and its embattled defenders. From this angle, he saw an Apache warrior about to heave another rock into the canyon.

Fargo snapped a shot at him, the bullet guided as much by instinct as by aim. The warrior cried out and fell backward, letting go of the rock. It dropped at his feet and remained on the rim.

Fargo shifted the Henry and fired again at another Apache who was trying to roll an even larger rock over the edge. The man slumped to the ground so that Fargo couldn't see him anymore, but the rock stopped moving.

Meanwhile, Olmsted, Glory, and Vangie kept up their fire toward the rim above Fargo. They would run out of ammunition eventually, but he knew they had a good supply. He watched the rim and fired twice more as Apaches approached the brink with rocks they intended to throw over. Each time, the warriors were forced to retreat.

Up above, a harsh voice shouted what sounded like orders. Fargo spoke a little of the Apache language, but he couldn't hear the words plainly enough to make them out. However, the shooting died away, and no more warriors approached the rim Fargo was covering. Fargo allowed himself to hope that the Apaches were pulling out, having encountered more resistance than they had expected.

"Hold your fire!" he called across to the others. As the echoes of the gunshots died away, a strained silence descended on the canyon.

After a moment, Olmsted asked, "Are they gone?"

"I think so," Fargo said, "but we'd better wait a while to make sure. Anybody hit over there?"

"No, we're all right, Skye," Vangie called back.

Fargo lay there among the rocks as the minutes stretched past. He knew from experience that an Apache could wait silently and motionlessly for hours in order to have the chance to strike at an enemy. The afternoon wore on. Fargo grew thirsty but ignored that as best he could. Finally, late in the afternoon, he stood up and moved out cautiously from the boulders. Across the creek, Olmsted emerged from behind the wagon. "Stay there, girls," the old man told his granddaughters.

No shots came from the rims as Fargo and Olmsted moved out into the open. They had a good look around and at last Fargo announced, "It looks like they're gone."

Olmsted tugged at his beard. "I'm thinkin' maybe this ain't such a good idea, Fargo. Maybe we should all go back to Gila City. It's too easy to get bottled up in this canyon."

"This is where the gold is," Glory protested.

Vangie said, "You just want to protect us, Gramps, but we don't want to leave. You've always dreamed of making a big strike."

"What good is a dream if the bloody Apaches lift your hair?" Olmsted shook his head. "We're goin' to have to abandon the diggin's, that's all there is to it."

The women continued to argue, but Olmsted was stubborn. Fargo stayed out of the discussion. It wasn't his decision to make. If Olmsted, Glory, and Vangie decided to stick it out here, he would do his best to help them. But if they wanted to gather the gold they had found so far and return to Gila City, he wouldn't try to dissuade them.

Finally, in exasperation, Olmsted turned toward the Trailsman and said, "What do you think we should do, Fargo?"

"It's too late to start back to the settlement today," Fargo pointed out. "I think you should sleep on it and make up your minds in the morning."

Olmsted scratched his head and said, "I reckon that's what we'll do. But I'm afraid there ain't no good answer."

Fargo thought he was probably right about that.

They had continued standing guard every night, rotating the shifts. That night, Fargo had the third shift, right after Vangie. Over the years he had developed the ability to wake up whenever he needed to, so he was awake before it came time for her to rouse him. He rolled out of his blankets, picked up the Henry from the ground beside him, and stood up to walk over to the wagon. Vangie was waiting for him.

"Everything's quiet," she told him in a whisper.

Fargo nodded. "Good. I didn't figure the Apaches would come back tonight, but you never know." He leaned against the wagon. "Go get some sleep. I'll take over now."

Vangie started to turn away, but then she stopped and said, "Skye, you made me a promise."

Fargo knew instantly what she was talking about. "This still isn't a good time," he said.

"There may not be a better time. You saw what happened yesterday. We might have been killed." She moved closer to him and went on in a soft voice, "I don't want to die without knowing what it's like to make love to you, Skye Fargo."

Her body was only inches from his. He seemed to feel the heat radiating from her, even through their clothes. She had a point, he thought. Life was fleeting, and a chance postponed was often a chance lost.

Besides, he could hear Olmsted snoring loudly in one tent, and Glory's tent was quiet and dark, too. She was probably sound asleep.

He put the Henry on the wagon seat and then slipped a hand behind Vangie's head. She tilted her face up to his as he leaned down to kiss her. When he took his lips away from hers, she whispered, "Thank you, Skye."

He smiled in the darkness. "I haven't really done anything yet."

"Oh, but you will. You surely will."

By unspoken, mutual agreement, they moved underneath the wagon. Fargo unbuttoned Vangie's shirt and spread it open, revealing her large, round, firm breasts. He bent his head to the left one and sucked

61

the hard nipple into his mouth. His tongue slid around the pebbled crown. Her skin tasted slightly salty. His teeth nipped the hard bud and drew a quiet gasp from her. He moved to her other breast and caressed the tip of it with lips and tongue and teeth, too.

Vangie worked at the buttons of her trousers and then lifted her hips so that she could push them down over her thighs. Fargo helped her get them off the rest of the way. Even in the deep shadows under the wagon, he could see the triangle of black hair between the fair skin of her spreading thighs. He trailed kisses down over her belly as he ran his fingers through the silky, luxuriant growth until he found the wet heat of her core.

He lowered his head even more and used his thumbs to open the fleshy folds. His tongue speared into her. Her hips bucked up off the ground as she bit back a cry of ecstasy. A low moan was the only sound that escaped her lips.

Fargo licked and stroked and caressed her for several minutes, until she was breathing hard and tugging at his shoulders. He kicked off the buckskin trousers and moved over her, positioning himself between her widespread thighs. She clutched at his erect manhood with both hands, gasping as she tried to wrap her fingers around the shaft. She brought the tip of it to her opening and dipped it into the heated moisture flowing from her.

"Now, Skye," she breathed. "Now!"

With a hard thrust of his hips, Fargo drove forward and sheathed himself inside her. Vangie met him with a thrust of her own, and they fell naturally into the eternal, universal rhythm of man and woman coupling.

Fargo felt his arousal growing as he pistoned in and out of her. The wet heat of her femininity surrounded him, clasping his shaft in a searing grip. The circumstances in which they found themselves gave their lovemaking an added urgency. This might be their first—and only—time. Fargo didn't try to hold back but rather gave her everything he had, freely and passionately.

She twined her arms around his neck and pulled his mouth down to hers. Their tongues dueled sensuously as her heels beat a tattoo on his driving hips. Fargo surged into her, penetrating her to the fullest, and they were as close together as two people could possibly be as their climaxes washed over them at the same moment.

Breathless, they held each other as they slid down the crest from the peak they had just shared. Fargo rolled onto his side and cuddled Vangie against him. His big, strong right hand came up and stroked her dark curls. "Thank you, Skye," she whispered again. "You don't know what this means to me."

"It means a lot to me, too," he told her.

"I just hope it won't be the last time. There's still *soooo* much I want to do with you."

Fargo laughed quietly and then kissed her again. "Hang on to that thought," he said. "It's always good to have something to look forward to."

The discussion—more of an argument, really—continued the next morning over breakfast, but in the end, the two young women couldn't budge Olmsted. He had made up his mind.

"Pack up the tents and everything else," he said. "We're leaving Skeleton Canyon."

"You know what's going to happen," Glory said bitterly. "Mahaffey and his friends are going to move in here and get rich."

"Perhaps," Olmsted admitted. "But if Rafaelito has his way, all they'll get is dead."

Vangie turned to Fargo. "Skye, can't you talk some sense into that old coot's head? He's turning his back on a fortune!"

"It's his decision to make," Fargo said.

"What about us?" Glory demanded. "Don't we have a stake in this, too?"

Olmsted shook his head. "The claim is registered in my name, as you well know, girls. If I want to abandon it, I can."

Seeing that he wasn't going to change his mind, the cousins finally gave up. There was still considerable grumbling going on, though, as everything was packed up and loaded onto the wagon, including the gold that the three of them had already taken out of the creek.

It was the middle of the morning before they were ready to leave. Fargo and Olmsted hitched up the mule team while Vangie and Glory took a last look around the campsite to make sure they weren't leaving anything behind. Then Olmsted climbed onto the seat and took the reins. Vangie and Glory both got in the back of the wagon, refusing to sit with their grandfather.

Fargo swung up onto the Ovaro's back and spoke quietly to the big stallion as he lifted the reins. He moved out in front of the wagon, his gaze darting back and forth from canyon rim to canyon rim, watching for any signs of an ambush. He didn't see anything unusual, but he suspected that Rafaelito was keeping an eye on the canyon and would know it when the whites left. Fargo hoped that the Apache war chief would realize they were pulling out for good and wouldn't try to jump the wagon on the way back to Gila City.

He emerged from the canyon and reined in, turning so that he could look past the wagon into the shadowy reaches of the gorge. From here, Fargo couldn't see the grave where they had buried the ancient skeleton, but he knew it was there. He couldn't help but wonder who the man had been and how he had come to be chained to the wall of that lonely cave. Some mysteries, though, Fargo knew would never be answered, and this was probably one of them.

Olmsted drove south along the trail that followed the Colorado River. No one bothered them. In fact, they didn't see another pilgrim all day, or anyone else until they reached the ferry just above the spot where the Colorado merged with the Gila River.

The ferrymen greeted them warmly and invited them to spend the night, but Olmsted shook his head. "There's still a bit of daylight left," he said. "I reckon we'll push on to Gila City."

Fargo paused the Ovaro beside the pipe-smoking ferrymen. "Seen anything of Flynn Pearsoll lately?" he asked quietly.

"Pearsoll and some of his pards rode by here a couple of days ago," one of the men replied. "They was headin' for town, looked like."

"Much obliged," Fargo said with a nod. He didn't know what Pearsoll had been up to while they were gone from Gila City, but the big redheaded hardcase was probably in the settlement now, and he might still be looking for trouble. That was good to know.

Fargo glanced across the Colorado River. Over there on the far shore lay California, his original destination. He could ride the stallion out onto the flat-bottomed ferry right now and pay the men to carry them across. But Olmsted, Glory, and Vangie were on their way to Gila City, and the potential threat of Flynn Pearsoll was too great for Fargo to ignore. He couldn't desert them until he was sure that they were reasonably safe.

He lifted a hand in farewell to the ferrymen and rode after the wagon.

When they got to Gila City, the settlement was as raucous as ever. Men strolled in the street and clogged the boardwalks as dusk gathered. Fargo looked for Flynn Pearsoll as he rode past the Pine Tree Saloon and Giddings's bathhouse, but he didn't see the man. He didn't know if Olmsted would go to the hotel first, or to the assayer's office. It turned out to be the latter.

Richmond, who ran the office, was a tall, paunchy man with an outthrust jaw. Fargo lounged in the doorway, one shoulder propped against the jamb, while Olmsted dumped a canvas bag full of nuggets onto the desk. Glory and Vangie added several leather pokes stuffed with gold dust.

The assayer looked at the gold and said, "It looks like you've got yourself a sure-enough strike, Bert."

Olmsted shook his head. "No, this is all of it," he said. "Just a fluke we found this much, I reckon. The claim's all played out."

Fargo knew what the old-timer was doing. Even though Olmsted was giving up now, he hadn't completely abandoned the idea of returning to the diggings at a later date when it might be safer to work the claim. In the meantime, his poor-mouthing was meant to keep anybody else from moving in. The ruse probably wouldn't work, Fargo reflected, but he supposed he couldn't blame the old man for trying.

"You want me to cash all this in?" Richmond asked.

"That's right. The girls and me are done, ain't we, girls?"

"Yeah," Vangie said listlessly. Glory just frowned.

Richmond got busy running his tests and measurements on the nuggets and weighing the dust. He said, "I'll sure miss you two ladies coming in to see me. You really brighten up a fella's day."

Glory ignored the compliment and said to her grandfather, "We're going over to the hotel, all right?"

"Sure, go ahead. I'll see you there in a bit."

Fargo moved out of the doorway and started to turn, thinking he would go to the hotel with the cousins, but Vangie put a hand on his arm and said quietly, "Skye, would you stay here and keep an eye on Gramps until he's finished? He'll be carrying quite a bit of money when he leaves."

Fargo considered for a second and then nodded. Vangie's suggestion was probably a good idea. Any boomtown had its share of cutthroats and robbers, and Gila City was no different. He would stay with Olmsted until they had the cash the old-timer received from the gold locked up securely in the hotel's safe.

It took a half hour for Richmond to finish his work

and calculate how much the gold was worth. He opened a safe underneath the desk and counted out the money to Olmsted in a mixture of bills and coins. It was a sizable amount, but only a fraction of what could be taken out of Skeleton Canyon if only it was safe to work the claim, Fargo thought. Still, for now Olmsted seemed satisfied with it.

Olmsted stuffed the cash into the bag that had held the nuggets. Hefting it, he turned toward the door and said to Fargo, "I could use a drink."

"Vangie and Glory are waiting for us over at the hotel," Fargo pointed out.

Olmsted wiped the back of his hand across his mouth. "I know that, but they'll be all right for a bit. I'm as thirsty as a man who's spent a month in the bloody Sahara, Fargo."

The Trailsman smiled. "All right, I guess it won't hurt anything for us to wet our whistles. Hang on tight to that bag, though."

"For dear life," Olmsted said as he clutched it to him.

It would have been all right with Fargo if they had gone to one of the smaller saloons, but Olmsted headed straight for the Pine Tree. That was where they were most likely to run into Pearsoll, Fargo thought, but when he said as much, Olmsted waved off the objection.

"The Pine Tree has the best whiskey in Gila City," the old-timer insisted. "Much better than the swill they serve in those other places."

Fargo didn't know about that, but he followed Olmsted, determined to keep the old prospector safe.

The atmosphere inside the Pine Tree was loud and smoky. Olmsted made a beeline for the bar as soon as he pushed past the batwings, but Fargo paused and looked around the room. He figured a big jigger like Flynn Pearsoll would be easy to spot. He didn't see the redhead, however.

But he saw Olmsted stop short and stiffen, and that

told him something was wrong. When Fargo stepped up beside him, Olmsted was staring at three men who stood at the bar.

The biggest of them must have felt Olmsted's gaze on him, because he glanced over his shoulder and then swung around. He was barrel-chested, around forty, with a rugged face and sandy hair under a broad-brimmed, flat-crowned hat. "Howdy, Olmsted," he greeted the Englishman.

"Mahaffey," Olmsted said curtly.

"Didn't expect to see you in town," Mahaffey said. The grin he gave Olmsted was indolent, mocking.

If this was Mahaffey, Fargo thought, then the other two would be his partners Jessel and Luman. Three would-be claim jumpers, according to Olmsted and his granddaughters. Fargo hadn't seen any proof of that, but he thought that the visit the three men had paid to Skeleton Canyon several nights earlier had been a mite suspicious. He wondered if Mahaffey and the others had planned on taking over the claim that night, only to find that Olmsted, Vangie, and Glory had returned to it.

The other two men turned to face Olmsted as well. One was slender, with a foxlike face, while the other was short and stocky and had a jagged white scar on his left cheek where somebody had slashed him with a knife. The slender one gave Olmsted an ugly grin and said, "Where's those pretty granddaughters of yours, old man? Didn't leave 'em by themselves out at those diggings, did you?"

"It ain't none of your business where Evangeline and Gloriana are, Jessel," Olmsted snapped.

"We just wouldn't want anything to happen to 'em," the short man put in. That would be Luman, Fargo noted.

None of them were paying any attention to him. They hadn't seen him the night they rode into the canyon, and evidently the way he had paused in the doorway of the saloon had kept them from realizing that he was with Olmsted. Fargo remedied that by stepping forward at a slight angle, so that he was between Olmsted and the three men. "Nothing's going to happen to those girls," he said quietly. "They're fine."

Mahaffey and the other two tensed. "Who the hell are you?" Mahaffey demanded.

"A friend of Bert's," Fargo replied, inclining his head toward Olmsted. His right hand rested on the butt of the Colt. "Name's Fargo."

"There's no call for you to horn in on this," Luman said angrily. "We were talkin' to the old man."

"I got nothin' to say to the likes of you," Olmsted said, "except good night and good-bye!"

"We're not going anywhere." Mahaffey's voice was low and dangerous.

"Well, then, I'm just going to pretend you ain't here." Olmsted stepped past them, heading for an open space at the bar. Fargo moved after him, watching the three men from the corner of his eye. Mahaffey, Jessel, and Luman stared after them, their faces dark with anger, but made no move to follow them and continue the confrontation.

Olmsted set his bag of money on the bar. Coins clinked inside it. "Whiskey, my good man," he said to the bartender. Fargo stood alongside him and nodded that he wanted the same.

Olmsted was right about the liquor. It went down smoothly and kindled a pleasant warmth in Fargo's belly. They had a couple of drinks. Fargo watched Mahaffey and the others in the mirror behind the bar, so he knew when the three men left the saloon.

"Better get on over to the hotel," he said quietly to Olmsted.

"I suppose you're right." Olmsted drained the rest of the amber liquid in his glass and smacked his lips in appreciation. He picked up the bag. "Shall we go?"

They went to the door. Fargo stepped through the batwings first and moved onto the boardwalk. Olmsted came up beside him. Fargo's nerves were taut and ready for trouble as he remembered how Mahaffey, Jessel, and Luman had left the Pine Tree first.

Side by side, they started across the street toward the hotel.

Fargo's keen hearing picked up the scrape of a foot and the metallic ratcheting of a gun being cocked. He pivoted swiftly, his left hand going out to shove Olmsted to the ground as his right swept down to the revolver at his hip. The Colt whispered out of gun leather as muzzle flame bloomed garishly orange in the darkness of an alley mouth beside the saloon.

Fargo heard the wind-rip of the bullet past his ear. The next instant the Colt bucked twice in his hand as he thumbed off a pair of shots and sent lead screaming into the alley. He dropped to a knee as he cocked the gun and fired again. More muzzle flashes split the shadows. Hoofbeats hammered in the night, coming closer. Fargo threw himself to the side as a horse loomed up and almost trampled him.

The rider was leading two horses with empty saddles. Fargo landed on his belly and loosed another round as two men hustled out of the alley and vaulted onto the riderless horses. They kicked the mounts into a gallop as they leaned far forward in the saddles, making smaller targets of themselves.

Olmsted was cursing sulfurously. Fargo picked himself up and hurried over to the old man, kneeling beside him. "Are you hit?" Fargo asked.

"No, but I think I wrenched my bloody knee when you pushed me down!"

Fargo's chuckle was grim. "Better that than a bullet in your gizzard."

"Did you see them? Did you hit any of the bastards?"

"I don't know. The two who bushwhacked us were moving pretty spry when they ran out of that alley and got on their horses."

"It was Mahaffey," Olmsted declared. "Mahaffey and those skunks who ride with him."

"More than likely," Fargo agreed as he grasped Olmsted's arm and helped the prospector to his feet. Olmsted gasped as he tried to put weight on his right leg. The limb folded up underneath him, and he would have fallen if not for Fargo's strong hand on his arm.

"I told you I hurt my knee!"

"So you did. Come on. If you can make it over to the hotel, we'll get you a room so you can lie down. I'm sure the girls will want to make a big fuss over you," Fargo added.

"As well they should," Olmsted sniffed.

Quite a few men had come out of the saloon to see what the shooting was about. One of them asked Fargo, "Does that old-timer need a sawbones, mister?"

"Probably wouldn't hurt, if you've got one."

"Sure, Doc Meader's office is down the street. I'll fetch him. You're going to the hotel?"

"That's right. Is there a marshal or any other law in this town?"

The man shook his head. "Nope, 'fraid not."

Fargo nodded. He didn't really care whether there was a star packer in Gila City or not. The bushwhackers were long gone, and no town marshal would have tried to track them down. In places like this, people took care of their own problems and settled their own legal disputes . . . usually with hot lead. That was fine with Fargo. He was already looking forward to his next meeting with Mahaffey, Jessel, and Luman.

Olmsted still hung on to the bag of money. He hadn't let go of it during the shooting scrape. Now Fargo put an arm around the old-timer and helped him hobble on across the street to the hotel. They made it onto the boardwalk and then inside, where they found the clerk watching wide-eyed out the front window.

"I heard all the shooting," the man said. "I was afraid a wild bullet was going to come in here."

"Reckon you were lucky," Fargo said. "My friend here needs a room, and somebody needs to tell his granddaughters that he's been hurt."

The clerk frowned in confusion. "You mean Miss Gloriana and Miss Evangeline?"

"Who else would he mean?" Olmsted demanded irritably. "Go fetch them gals!"

The man blinked rapidly. "I . . . I'm afraid I can't, Mr. Olmsted. I know your granddaughters, and I haven't seen them. They haven't been in here all night."

6

Fargo and Olmsted both stared at the clerk. After a couple of seconds, Olmsted demanded, "What do you mean they ain't been in here?"

The clerk looked confused and apologetic. "I'm sorry, Mr. Olmsted, but I haven't seen them. Were they supposed to be here?"

"They said they were coming here when they left the assayer's office," Fargo explained. He turned to Olmsted. "There's not another hotel in Gila City where they might have gone, is there?"

The old-timer shook his head. "I doubt it. This is where we stayed when we first came here, while we were outfittin' ourselves to head up the Colorado and look for gold. I'm sure this is where they meant to come."

Fargo was fairly confident of that fact himself, confident enough that he could think of only one reasonable explanation for Glory and Vangie not being here.

Something had happened to them along the way.

Obviously, the same thought had occurred to Olmsted. "We've got to find them!" he exclaimed. He turned and took a hurried step toward the front door of the hotel—

And fell heavily to the floor as his injured leg went out from under him.

Fargo hadn't had time to grab the old man's arm and steady him. Olmsted had moved with surprising speed. Now Fargo knelt beside Olmsted as the worried clerk rushed over to them.

"Get him into a room and put him to bed," Fargo told the clerk. "His leg's hurt and he needs to rest."

"So it's rest I need, is it?" Olmsted raged. "The only reason I'm hurt is because you pushed me down!"

"To keep you from getting shot or trampled," Fargo reminded the old prospector as he helped him to his feet. To the clerk, the Trailsman added, "The doctor's supposed to be on his way here to have a look at that leg."

The clerk nodded and took Olmsted's other arm. "I'll see that he's taken care of."

"Don't talk about me like I ain't even here!"

Fargo ignored Olmsted's protests and swung toward the entrance. He had to find Glory and Vangie, or at least find out where they had gone. Minutes might be of the essence to their safety.

He left the hotel and headed for the assayer's office. A light still burned there. Richmond worked late, not uncommon for an assayer in a boomtown.

The jut-jawed man looked up from his desk as Fargo came into the office. They had been introduced briefly before. Richmond nodded and said, "Mr. Fargo. I didn't expect to see you back here tonight."

"Didn't expect to be here," Fargo said. "Have you seen Glory and Vangie?"

"Olmsted's granddaughters?" Richmond shook his head. "Not since they left here a while ago, if that's what you mean."

"Since Olmsted and I were here?"

Again a shake of the assayer's head. "No. I'm talking about when they left to go over to the hotel, while you and Bert were still here."

"They never got there."

Richmond's forehead creased in a worried frown. "You don't know where they are?"

"No."

"That's not good. Gila City can be a pretty rough place, especially after dark. Why, I heard some shooting up the street just a little while ago."

Fargo didn't waste time explaining that he knew all about the shooting—he and Olmsted had been in the middle of it. Instead he nodded curtly, said, "Thanks," and turned back to the door.

"If there's anything I can do to help . . ." Richmond called after him, but Fargo didn't respond to the offer. He was already thinking about where else to check for the two young women.

His long strides took him toward the livery stable where they had left the wagon, the mules, and the Ovaro. When they weren't busy, the hostlers often sat out in front of the barn, watching the goings-on in town. They might have seen something.

When he walked up, one of the hostlers surprised him by saying, "Howdy, Mr. Fargo. Come to get that big black-and-white horse of yours?"

Fargo frowned. "No. What makes you think I would be?"

"Well, Miss Glory and Miss Vangie said you might be along later to get him."

"When did they say this?" Fargo asked sharply.

"Why, just about an hour ago, I reckon."

That would have been right after they left the assayer's office, Fargo thought.

"When they picked up their grandfather's wagon," the hostler added.

"They got the wagon?"

"Sure. The fellas and I hitched up the mules for 'em, even though they said they could do it themselves. Those gals are mighty self-reliant, as well as mighty pretty." The man suddenly looked worried as a thought occurred to him. "Say, I didn't do anything wrong by letting them have the wagon, did I? I figured since they're always with Mr. Olmsted, it'd be all right. And they said you might be along later, and here you are."

Fargo drew a deep breath. Here he was, all right, and he had found a new conclusion staring him in the face. Judging by what he had just heard, nothing had happened to Glory and Vangie, and they weren't in any trouble. They had gotten the wagon and left Gila City on their own.

"Did you see which way they went?" he asked quietly.

"They took the road west out of town, toward the Colorado."

Fargo nodded, his suspicions confirmed by the answer. Glory and Vangie had been opposed to leaving the diggings in the first place, and now they had taken things into their own hands.

They were going back to Skeleton Canyon.

"Much obliged," Fargo said. "Get my horse ready to ride."

"Tonight?"

"You didn't mind when those girls drove off in the dark by themselves," Fargo snapped.

The hostler looked abashed. "Yes, sir. We'll get that horse of yours ready right away."

Fargo headed for the hotel. Bert Olmsted had to be told what had happened.

When he came in, the clerk was back behind the desk but still looked worried. "Did you find them?" he asked Fargo.

"Not yet. Where's Olmsted?"

"Up in room seven, right at the top of the stairs. Doc Meader is with him now."

Fargo nodded and started up, taking the stairs two at a time. He didn't pause to knock on the door of room seven, just opened it and went inside.

A middle-aged man with brown hair and a beard was straightening from the bed, where he had just finished wrapping bandages tightly around Bert Olmsted's right knee. "You need to stay off that leg as much as possible for several days," he said. "It would be better if you'd take it easy for a week."

"The hell with that!" Olmsted said as he tried to

sit up. The doctor's firm hand on his shoulder pressed him back down.

Meader glanced over his shoulder at Fargo. "Are you a friend of his?"

"That's right," Fargo replied as he stepped forward.

"Then you should impress upon him the need to follow my orders, or else he's liable to damage that knee even worse and never be able to walk again."

Olmsted ignored the doctor's solemn warning. "Did you find them?" he demanded of Fargo.

"No, but I've got a pretty good idea where they are. They went back over to the livery stable after they left Richmond's office."

"The livery stable! Why would they do that?"

"So they could get the wagon and the mules and head back out to Skeleton Canyon."

Olmsted's head sagged against the pillow under it as he stared open-mouthed at Fargo. After a few seconds, he recovered from his surprise enough to speak. "Back to camp? Good Lord, why?"

"You know the answer to that as well as I do," Fargo said.

Olmsted glanced at the doctor and said, "Yeah, I reckon I do." Meader was probably pretty closemouthed—most small-town physicians were—but Olmsted didn't want to talk too much about the gold in front of him. No point in taking chances; that was the way he would look at it.

"I'll go after them," Fargo said. "The hostler over at the livery stable is saddling my horse right now."

Again Olmsted tried to sit up. "I'm going with you."

This time it was Fargo who stepped up beside the bed and stopped him with a hand on the shoulder. "No, you're not. Listen to the doc and do what he tells you. I can move faster by myself."

Olmsted glowered up from the bed, but Fargo's argument seemed to make sense to him. He said grudgingly, "All right. You reckon you can follow the trail at night?"

The Trailsman smiled faintly. "I can manage. And I can move a lot faster than they can in that wagon. It shouldn't take me long to catch up to them."

"Bring 'em back here when you do. And if they won't come along, you've my permission to spank those little minxes!"

Fargo didn't imagine the idea of a spanking would sit too well with Glory and Vangie. They might surprise him, though.

"Just rest and don't worry," he told Olmsted. "I'll get back here with them as quick as I can."

Olmsted sighed. "Thanks, Fargo. I don't really know why you got mixed up with me and mine to start with, but I'm glad you did."

"Just trying to lend a hand," Fargo said. He looked at the doctor. "You'll keep an eye on him until I get back?"

Meader nodded. "I'll check on him as often as I can."

"Much obliged." Fargo turned and stalked out of the room without wasting any more time.

The Ovaro was ready when he got back to the stable. The big black-and-white stallion had been saddled and led out, and the hostler Fargo had spoken to earlier stood there holding the reins. As the man handed them over, he said, "I sure hope you find those gals, Mr. Fargo. I took the liberty of puttin' some jerky in your saddlebags, just in case you get a mite hungry before you get back, and I filled your canteen, too."

Fargo nodded his thanks and swung up into the saddle. He put the Ovaro into a fast lope that took him along the western trail out of town.

When he reached the Colorado River, he saw that the shack where the ferrymen lived was dark. He rode up next to it, leaned over, and banged a fist on the door. "Wake up!" he called.

As Fargo backed the horse away a few steps, the door swung open and an angry voice said, "We ain't makin' any more trips across tonight. Come back in the mornin'."

"I'm not taking the ferry," Fargo said. "I want to know if you heard a wagon go by here a while ago."

The man stepped out into the moonlight, using the knuckles of his right hand to rub his eyes. He had a shotgun tucked under his left arm. He blinked up at Fargo and said, "Hey, mister, I remember you."

"What about the wagon?" Fargo asked, in no mood right now for small talk.

The ferryman scratched his head. "Not me. I was asleep." He turned and called into the shack, "Tom, come out here!"

The other ferryman stumbled out of the shack a moment later. "What the hell's all the commotion?" he asked irritably.

"You hear a wagon go by earlier?"

"Earlier tonight, you mean?"

"That's right."

Fargo's jaw tightened in impatience. He was about to lash out verbally at the two ferrymen, when the second one said, "Come to think of it, I did. About an hour ago, I reckon, just before I dozed off. I remember thinkin' it was odd to hear a wagon go by at night like this."

Fargo jerked a thumb toward the north. "Was it headed along the river?"

The second ferryman nodded. "From the sound of it, I'd say it was."

"Thanks," Fargo said. He swung the Ovaro onto the trail that followed the Colorado and heeled the stallion into a trot.

One of the ferrymen called after him, "Better be careful! Could be Apaches around!"

Fargo didn't acknowledge the warning, but the same thought had occurred to him. A lot of dangers could be abroad this night, including not only Rafaelito's band of warriors but also Mahaffey, Jessel, and

Luman, and Flynn Pearsoll, too. Glory and Vangie had taken their lives in their hands by starting back to Skeleton Canyon alone and in the dark.

Fargo kept the stallion moving at a ground-eating pace. The moon was only a quarter full, but that was enough light for the keen eyes of the Trailsman. In places he could even see the fresh ruts left in the dust by the wagon wheels.

It had been a long day and weariness began to overtake him after he had ridden for an hour or so, but his iron constitution enabled him to ignore it and push on. Glory and Vangie might make it back to Skeleton Canyon without encountering any trouble, but he couldn't count on that.

And when he heard distant popping sounds a short time later, he knew that faint hope had disappeared. Those noises were gunshots, and for several moments they came fast and furious.

Fargo bit back a curse and put the Ovaro into a gallop as the shots died away.

He rode hard, trusting to the big stallion's instincts. The Ovaro avoided rough places in the trail and kept up the lunging pace. Fargo paused only occasionally to listen. He didn't hear any more shots, and that silence wasn't a good thing. More than likely, it meant that Glory and Vangie weren't able to put up a fight anymore.

Time seemed to slow, stretching out maddeningly. Fargo rode and rode but didn't seem to be getting anywhere. At last he spotted a faint orange glow in the sky up ahead. That wasn't a good sign, either. Something was on fire up there.

He came around a bend in the trail and saw flames dying down around the wreckage of the wagon. The vehicle lay on its side. As he approached, still at a gallop, his eyes searched the ground for any sign of Glory and Vangie, but he didn't see them. The mules were gone, too.

He pulled the Henry from its saddle sheath and

then leaped to the ground even before the Ovaro had come to a halt. He twisted from side to side as he ran forward, ready to fight if any of the Apaches were still around. He was fairly certain that Rafaelito was responsible for this attack. It was unlikely that white men would have burned the wagon. Apaches, on the other hand, wouldn't have any use for it.

The dying flames provided enough light so that Fargo was sure Glory and Vangie weren't there. He saw some dark splotches on the ground that were probably blood, but he had no way of knowing if it had belonged to them or to the Apaches. The two young women had put up a fight, Fargo was sure of that. He had heard the shots with his own ears.

"Glory!" Fargo shouted. "Vangie!" He repeated the names several times, but there was no response except for the echoes of his own shouts rolling back to him.

They were gone. Fargo had no idea how badly they were hurt, or even if they were still alive. The only thing he knew for sure was that they had been taken by the Apaches.

Following the trail of a wagon by moonlight was one thing; following a band of Apache warriors was entirely another. The Indians would try to conceal their trail. Fargo knew he stood no chance of tracking Rafaelito's band until daylight. All he could hope for was that Glory and Vangie were still alive and that they would be kept as prisoners for the moment, rather than being raped or tortured to death right away.

Fargo moved several hundred yards from the burned-out remains of the wagon, just in case any of the Apaches returned to it during the night, and found a place to throw his bedroll. The stallion would alert him if anyone came around. He crawled into his blankets, pillowed his head on his saddle, and went to sleep almost immediately, something most frontiersmen learned to do. A man never knew when he might have the chance to sleep again, so he had to take advantage of the opportunities that came his way.

Fargo woke well before dawn. He had no coffee, but he made do with jerky and water from his canteen for a cold breakfast. As soon as the sky had turned gray enough for him to be able to see, he saddled up and rode out, moving slowly so that he wouldn't overlook anything.

It took almost an hour of searching before he picked up the Apaches' trail. He finally found a few threads of blue cloth on the spine of a cactus where someone had brushed up against it, and a few minutes later he came across half a footprint in the sand. That pointed him in the right direction. The signs left behind by the warriors were few and far between, but they were enough for the Trailsman.

The trail led into the rugged foothills of the mountains that rose to the east of the river. This was an arid land, full of rocky red outcroppings, bone-dry arroyos, and stark mesas. Here and there were springs and pockets of green grass, bordered by scrubby trees. A man could graze a few cattle here, but man and animal alike would have to be hardy breeds. Farming was out of the question. The land's real value lay in the minerals that could be found there, but finding them and getting them out was a challenge. Still, there was no shortage of wealth seekers trying to answer that challenge, even though they had to risk their lives to do so. Call them Arizona argonauts, always seeking that elusive golden fleece, Fargo mused as he rode through the increasingly hot morning.

He lost the trail several times and had to backtrack until he picked it up again. Every delay chafed at him and increased his worry about Glory and Vangie. Of course, some people would say he was on a fool's errand anyway, he thought. Chances were the girls were already dead. Even if they weren't, what were the odds against him being able to snatch them away from Rafaelito's band?

Fargo didn't know the answer to that, but he knew he couldn't just ride away and leave them to their fates. Besides, he had prevailed against some pretty stiff odds on occasion in the past. Maybe his luck hadn't deserted him yet.

The trail climbed higher and twisted around the base of a red sandstone butte. As Fargo followed it, he suddenly smelled a faint tinge of woodsmoke in the air. He reined the Ovaro to a halt.

The smoke meant only one thing: he was near a camp. The only ones likely to be camped out here in this wilderness were the Apaches. Fargo swung down from the saddle, left the stallion with the reins dangling, and went forward silently on foot, ghosting along the base of the butte.

He heard a horse whicker somewhere up ahead. Pausing, he looked around and saw an almost invisible trail that ran up the side of the butte to his left, while the main trail curved on around the promontory. Fargo started to climb, using tiny handholds and footholds that a man with lesser eyesight probably never would have noticed. The smoothness of the rock under his fingertips told him that men had used this path in the past, probably pretty often.

The landscape fell away to his right in an awe-inspiring vista. Fargo wasn't in any mood to appreciate the scenery, though. He had to concentrate on what he was doing, because if he slipped and fell, he would be badly injured at best, and more than likely killed by the plunge. As he climbed, he spotted a tendril of smoke rising above the butte. He didn't believe the Apache camp was on top of the butte, which meant it was somewhere on the far side. He ought to have a good view of it from the top, once he got there.

Finally, he pulled himself over the edge onto a relatively level stretch of ground. The top of the butte was a rough circle several hundred yards across. Tufts of grass growing here and there were the only vegetation. Fargo paused for a moment to catch his breath after the tough climb, then started toward the far side, moving in a low crouch.

He could see that he had been right about the smoke. It rose from a campfire on the other side of the butte. Fargo took off his hat and dropped to his hands and knees before he got to the edge. He went to his belly as he approached the rim and crawled forward. Down below, a man said something, and another man answered, their voices plain in the hot, clear air.

Fargo stayed as low as he could as he risked a look over the brink. He saw that his guess had been correct. A little valley lay between the butte and the steep slope of a hill. The place was watered by a spring that fed a small creek lined with cottonwoods. In the scorching landscape, this was a hidden oasis, and the Apaches, of course, knew about it, making their camp there and building hogans along the creek. Fargo saw a few women and children moving around, and a couple of warriors sat in the shade of a cottonwood and cleaned their rifles. A rope corral nearby held a few horses.

Fargo looked for Glory and Vangie but didn't see any sign of them. After a few minutes, a man emerged from one of the hogans and strode toward the two who were sitting under the cottonwood. He was fairly tall for an Apache and wore crossed bandoliers of ammunition over his loose blue shirt. He spoke sharply to the other two men, and Fargo guessed he was looking at Rafaelito, the war chief of this band.

The two warriors under the tree set their rifles aside and got up to follow the third man. They all went back to the hogan, and when they came out a few moments later, they brought Glory and Vangie with them. Fargo's heart thudded heavily in his chest when he saw that the two young women were alive. Their clothes were ripped and their faces were marked with bruises and scratches, but neither of them seemed to be badly hurt. They were scared, though. Fargo could tell that from their pale, tightly drawn faces. But they were trying not to show it, and they lifted their chins defiantly as Rafaelito spoke to them.

Fargo could follow enough of the talk to be able to tell that the war chief was threatening Glory and Vangie with torture. Rafaelito lapsed into Spanish when they had trouble understanding him. Fargo heard the word *viejo*—old fool—and figured Rafaelito was talking about Bert Olmsted. Rafaelito said something about a canyon—Skeleton Canyon, Fargo supposed—and added a vehement statement about *El Diablo*, then something about a *monstruo* and a *maledicion*.

The Devil, a monster, and a curse . . . what the hell was he talking about? Fargo wondered. It had to have something to do with Skeleton Canyon, of course, and despite the heat of midday, Fargo felt a chill go through him as he remembered those dusty old bones he had found chained to the wall inside the cave.

Rafaelito continued haranguing Glory and Vangie. Fargo translated the talk as best he could in his mind and realized to his surprise that Rafaelito was trying to extract a promise from them that they would never go back to the canyon. The war chief didn't come right out and say it, but Fargo sensed that he might be willing to let them go if they would just agree.

Unfortunately, they were being stubborn. Vangie shook her head and said in Spanish, "You just want the place for yourself."

Rafaelito drew back as if she had slapped him. He muttered something about a curse again.

Fargo frowned. He wondered if Olmsted and the two young women had really understood the situation as well as they thought they had. They had said that the Apaches considered Skeleton Canyon sacred ground. Maybe what Rafaelito had meant was that the canyon was cursed, rather than sacred. And those Old

85

Ones, whose spirits haunted the place, were not the Apaches' ancestors, but some sort of monsters instead.

Fargo wasn't sure he believed in monsters, although he had seen some strange things during his wanderings, things that maybe couldn't be completely explained. But the longer he listened to Rafaelito's ranting, the more convinced he was that the Apache leader believed *something* in Skeleton Canyon was evil and should not be disturbed.

The faint scuff of leather on rock behind him was all the warning Fargo had. He let his instincts take over and rolled hard to one side. As he came onto his back he saw an Apache warrior leaping at him, knife poised for a killing stroke.

7

Now that he had been discovered, the Apache no longer had any reason to keep silent. He let out a bloodcurdling cry as the knife plunged down at Fargo. The Trailsman kept rolling, so that the cold steel missed him and struck the ground instead. At the same moment, Fargo swept a leg out and knocked the Apache's feet out from under him. The warrior fell heavily.

Fargo was on him in a flash, his left hand gripping the Apache's right wrist and pinning it to the ground. Fargo's right palmed out the Colt and struck with it. The barrel thudded against the Apache's skull, and the man went limp underneath Fargo. Fargo had no desire to kill the warrior, but he felt no guilt about clouting him, either.

The problem was that this warrior wasn't alone. With shrill cries, several more Apaches rushed at Fargo from the far side of the butte, where they must have climbed up the same dim path he had used.

He came up on one knee, leveled the Colt, and fired a shot above their heads. That made them veer apart from each other, but they didn't stop coming. There were three of them, Fargo saw now, and two were armed with rifles. One of that pair stopped and took a shot at him. The bullet whistled past Fargo's head as he ducked to the side.

Shouts came from the camp down below. The fat

was really in the fire now. Outnumbered, with no place to hide and no place to run, Fargo had little chance to escape. But he had never been in the habit of giving up, and he didn't intend to start now.

The two with rifles represented the biggest threat. From a crouch, Fargo fired, putting a bullet through the arm of one of the men. The Apache cried out, dropped his rifle, and clutched the injured limb. A bullet from the other man's rifle chipped rock at Fargo's feet as the Trailsman shifted his aim and fired again. This slug caught the second Apache in the thigh and sent him spinning off his feet.

That left the third man, who charged straight on at Fargo, brandishing a knife. Fargo intended to wound him, too, but just as he fired, the first man who had attacked him regained his senses and grabbed Fargo's leg. The heave threw Fargo off-balance and sent the bullet screaming harmlessly into the sky.

Fargo caught his balance and used his other leg to kick the Apache loose. The man slumped back, stunned again. The other one had time to close in, though, and Fargo used the Colt to desperately parry the thrust of the knife. Blade and barrel clashed loudly.

Fargo swung a left into the Apache's body, smashing his fist hard against the man's midsection. The warrior's momentum carried him into Fargo anyway. The collision sent them both down. They landed dangerously close to the edge of the butte.

Somehow, Fargo hung on to the Colt. He lashed out with it again. The Apache ducked his head and took the blow on his shoulder, crying out in pain. He dropped the knife from fingers that must have gone numb. His other arm still worked, though, and he used it to grapple with Fargo. As he got his hand on Fargo's neck, he lifted a knee to the Trailsman's groin as well.

Agony flooded through Fargo's body. He doubled over as waves of black and red rolled through his brain. Instinct kept him fighting. He drove his knee into the Apache's belly, then struck again with the revolver. This time the blow landed squarely on the man's head.

Panting, Fargo forced himself to his feet. He staggered a little, caught his balance, and then started toward the other side of the butte, hoping he could climb down and make it to the Ovaro before the rest of the warriors cut him off.

That was a futile hope, he saw a second later. He had taken only a couple of steps when another warrior appeared at the top of the path. He scrambled up and leveled a rifle at Fargo. Another Apache followed him, then another and another, and in less than half a minute, six cold-eyed warriors stood there with their rifles lined up on the buckskin-clad white man.

Fargo sighed. He couldn't hope to down all of them, and even if he dropped a couple of the Apaches, those who were left would shoot him to pieces. As long as Glory and Vangie were still alive, he had to preserve his own life, too, in hopes of getting all of them free later on.

"All right, you've got me," Fargo said, not knowing if any of the Apaches spoke English. They would understand, though, when he bent over and placed his Colt on the ground at his feet. He drew the Arkansas Toothpick and dropped it next to the revolver. His Henry was still down below on the saddle. No doubt the Apaches had it, along with the Ovaro, by now, although it was possible the stallion had broken away and not allowed himself to be captured. Fargo hoped that was the case.

Another Apache appeared at the top of the path. The others stepped aside for him. Rafaelito strode toward Fargo, his face as cold and hard as flint.

"The other man from the accursed canyon," Rafaelito said in Spanish.

"Why do you say it's cursed?" Fargo asked. Even in this desperate situation, he wanted to learn more about the mysteries of Skeleton Canyon.

Rafaelito seemed to be in no mood to explain, though. He made a curt gesture and said to his warriors in the Apache tongue, "Take him down to the camp."

Men moved to either side of Fargo and grabbed his arms. They shoved him toward the far side of the butte while other men picked up the Colt and the Arkansas Toothpick. Fargo didn't try to put up a fight. There was a time and a place for that, and this was neither.

With men above him and men below him, he was forced to climb down the steep path to the trail where he had left the Ovaro. Fargo looked around for the stallion but didn't see him. He hoped that meant the big horse had taken off rather than let himself be captured. The Ovaro would stay close by, waiting to see if Fargo escaped from the Indians.

Fargo and his captors walked the rest of the way around the butte and entered the little valley where the Apache camp was located. He didn't see Glory and Vangie, but he noted that a couple of warriors were standing outside the hogan where the young women had been earlier. Fargo guessed that they had been put back in there when the commotion broke out on top of the butte overlooking the camp.

There must have been a sentry somewhere who had spotted him climbing up, he thought. He had checked, but not even a trailsman could see everything. He hoped that oversight wouldn't cost his life, along with those of Glory and Vangie.

Rafaelito came to a stop, and so did everyone else. The war chief barked in guttural Apache, "Get the women." A minute later, Glory and Vangie were led from the hogan. Fargo was relieved to see that they were still unhurt.

"Skye!" they cried out simultaneously when they saw him. They would have rushed forward, but their arms were being held by the guards. As they were brought up beside him, Vangie asked, "Skye, what are you doing here?"

"Looking for you two, of course," he replied. "You didn't really think that your grandfather and I would just sit there in Gila City after you ran out on us, did you?"

Glory looked around worriedly. "Where is Gramps? Is he here, too?"

They were speaking in English, and judging by the way Rafaelito was scowling darkly at them, he didn't understand the language and didn't like them talking to each other. Before the war chief could put a stop to the conversation, Fargo said quickly, "Bert's all right. He's back in the settlement with a sprained knee. Couldn't ride."

"Enough!" Rafaelito commanded in Spanish. "Talk to me, white man."

Fargo faced him calmly. "What do you want of us?"

"What I want is for you and all the other white men to go back where you came from and leave this land to the Apache." Rafaelito's scowl darkened. "But since I think you will not do this, I want you to stay away from the canyon of the Old Ones."

"Skeleton Canyon," Fargo said.

"Your people call it that. They know not its true name . . . or anything about the curse that lays upon it."

Since Rafaelito didn't seem inclined to start torturing them right away, Fargo thought it might be a good idea to keep the war chief talking. "Tell me what you mean," he said.

Rafaelito shook his head. "Not yet." He spoke in Apache, issuing commands in a quick, harsh tone that Fargo had trouble understanding. He picked up the word "stakes," though. A moment later he got a bad feeling as he saw several warriors begin to pound sharpened wooden stakes into the ground. Maybe he had been too hasty in his assumption that Rafaelito didn't intend to torture them.

91

Several of the Apaches grabbed Glory and Vangie. They screamed and tried to fight back, but there were too many of the warriors. Fargo's jaw tightened in anger and he took an involuntary step forward as the Apaches began ripping the clothes off the young women. Before Fargo could swing a punch, the barrel of a rifle dug painfully into his back and another one was aimed at his face. He had no choice but to control the fury he felt coursing through him.

"Your time is coming, white man," Rafaelito said.

The Indians didn't have rape in mind, at least not yet. They stripped Glory and Vangie naked and threw them on the ground, grabbing their thrashing arms and legs and using rawhide thongs to tie them to the stakes. The young women were spread out in the brutal sun.

When the Apaches were finished with Glory and Vangie, Fargo got the same treatment. A rifle butt was slammed into the back of his head first, so that he was too stunned to put up a fight as the warriors tore his buckskins off and staked him out. The sun stabbed cruelly at his eyes. It was almost directly overhead, and the heat was staggering. Where Fargo and the girls were staked out, there would be no shade until very late in the day.

By then they would be out of their heads and ready to die, Fargo thought. If Rafaelito left them there that long . . .

He closed his eyes. A few feet away, Glory and Vangie whimpered and cried as the sun burned their fair skin. Fargo wanted to tell them to be quiet and not give the Apaches the satisfaction of seeing how much pain they were in. But that was too much to expect of them, he told himself. They had never undergone an ordeal such as this. Fargo had. The fact that he was still here, that he had survived things like this—and worse—was reason enough for him not to give up hope.

Long minutes passed as the sun burned down. Fargo

lost track of time and didn't really know how long they had been out there. He opened his eyes as Rafaelito finally spoke again. The war chief's voice was close. Fargo saw that he was hunkering on his heels only a few feet from the prisoners. The other warriors had drawn back several steps into the shade under the trees, but they were still watching. The two Fargo had wounded seemed to be taking particular pleasure in witnessing what was going on. Their injuries had been bound up, and they leered at the captives.

"You want to know the story of the canyon of the Old Ones and why they must not be disturbed," Rafaelito began. "Listen and I will tell you, and let the heat of the sun burn the truth of my words into your hearts and souls. Then you will understand."

"Go on," Fargo said. "I'm listening."

"The Apache were not the first people to live in this land. There were others here, long before us."

Fargo knew that. The Apaches had come from what was now Texas. As fierce as they were, in times past they had encountered even more ferocious warriors in the Comanche, who had drifted south from the Great Plains. The Comanches had forced the Apaches ever westward, until now there were only a few enclaves of them left in far West Texas and across the Rio Grande in Mexico.

"But those who lived here were not people like us," Rafaelito went on.

That was a commonly held opinion among Indian tribes. Many of the tribes' names translated as meaning "The People" or "The Real People." Everyone who was not a member of the tribe was considered somehow less than human. That was one way they justified the constant warfare and taking of slaves between the tribes.

Somehow, though, as Fargo looked at and listened to Rafaelito, he got the feeling that wasn't exactly what the war chief meant.

"These Old Ones, the ones who came before, wore

the skins of men but were not men. When they wanted to, they could shed the skins of men and reveal the monsters underneath. And they lived only to kill. When our people came here, many of them were killed by the Old Ones.''

Fargo was interested enough in the story that he didn't notice the heat quite as much now. Glory and Vangie were still suffering considerably, though, and Fargo hoped Rafaelito wouldn't take too long in telling them what he wanted them to know. He hoped as well that once the story was finished, Rafaelito would order that they be released from this torment.

"The Apache fought back,'' Rafaelito said, anger and defiance at this ancient threat evident in his voice. "The Old Ones could not be defeated by normal means. It took powerful medicine to slay them, but eventually our people learned how to use that medicine, and over time the Old Ones were killed. All except one.''

Fargo frowned as he began to get an idea where this yarn was headed. "The skeleton in the canyon . . .'' he began.

Rafaelito nodded. "The last of the Old Ones. The strongest one of all. He was brought low by the powers of the Apache medicine men, but they were unable to slay him. So they left him in the canyon where they caught him, chained to the wall of a cave, hoping that sooner or later his life would come to an end. And as long as his bones molder there, that canyon will be forever cursed, and no Apache will ever set foot in it.''

Fargo thought it wise not to mention the fact that he and Olmsted and the girls had taken the skeleton from the cave and buried it. It was likely the Apaches would regard such a disturbance of the bones as sacrilege.

A moment later, he knew his hunch was right, because Rafaelito concluded by saying, "The legends of our people say that if the last of the Old Ones is ever released from its bondage, it will return to bring death

94

and destruction to us. That is why no one should be in the canyon, ever. There is great danger there, not only to anyone who would enter it, but also to the Apache people."

"I understand what you say, Rafaelito," Fargo said. Bert Olmsted had already abandoned the mining claim, so Fargo had no trouble promising, "If you release us, we will not return to the canyon."

"You give me your word, white man?"

"I do."

"Why should I believe you? Your people have always lied to mine."

"I don't," Fargo said. "I have met the Apache before, and always I have spoken the truth to them. My name is Skye Fargo." He didn't know if it was a trump card or not, but he played it anyway. The sun was really getting bad.

"Fargo," Rafaelito repeated. "Fargo. I have heard this name. It is said that it belongs to an honest man."

"I'd like to think so."

"You will not return to the canyon of the Old Ones?"

"No."

The war chief gave a curt nod, then lifted his head and spoke to the warriors. A couple of them came forward and began cutting the rawhide thongs that bound the captives to the wooden stakes. Fargo closed his eyes for a second in relief as his arms and legs were freed and the taut muscles were allowed to relax. His hands and feet had gone numb. They prickled painfully as the blood began to flow in them again.

He rolled onto his side and saw that Glory and Vangie had passed out from the ordeal. Apaches warriors lifted them, carried them toward the hogan where they had been kept earlier. Men stepped forward to help Fargo get to his feet, but he motioned them back and Rafaelito nodded. With an effort, Fargo pushed himself upright and stumbled after them.

The shaded interior of the hogan was blessedly cool

after the inferno of being staked out in the sun. Fargo knew that his skin was blistered, and so was that of the two young women. The burns might not be too bad, though. Glory and Vangie had been placed on blankets spread on the ground. Fargo sank down cross-legged beside them. Through the open entrance of the hogan, he could see warriors standing guard. He and the girls were still prisoners.

A couple of Apache women came in with clay pots. The pots contained a concoction that appeared to be made of mud and ground-up roots and the juice from a plant. The women daubed it on the blistered skin of Glory and Vangie. Fargo took one of the pots and rubbed the stuff on himself. It cooled him almost immediately.

Another woman brought in a gourd full of water. Fargo drank thirstily but forced himself to stop before he guzzled down all of the liquid. He reached over and got an arm under Glory's shoulders so that he could lift her head and hold the gourd to her lips. He dribbled water into her mouth. She choked a little but swallowed most of it. Fargo did the same for Vangie, then drank more of the water himself.

Under the circumstances, the fact that they were all nude meant very little. Still, Fargo was a man, and as such he noted the firm breasts, the appealing curves of their hips, Glory's long, coltish legs and Vangie's more muscular ones. Both women were beautiful, even sunburned and daubed with mud as they were. Fargo smiled faintly as his manhood began to swell. One of the Apache women noticed it, too, and pointed it out to her companion, her eyes widening in appreciation. Their attention made Fargo a mite uncomfortable, but he grinned anyway. The women left, talking to each other and laughing. One of them held up her hands a good distance apart and nodded enthusiastically.

Considering how Apache women sometimes treated prisoners, Fargo figured he had gotten off mighty lightly.

He turned back to Glory and Vangie. They were starting to come around, stirring a little on the blankets and fluttering their eyelids. After a few more minutes, Glory opened her eyes and gasped. Fargo leaned over and said quietly, "It's all right, Glory. It's over now."

"Skye . . . ?" She lifted a hand. Fargo caught hold of it with both of his and squeezed in reassurance. Glory closed her eyes and sighed. "Oh, Skye, I thought I was being burned alive out there."

"It was a mite rough for a while," Fargo said. "But you'll be fine. You're blistered some, but that'll heal."

"Vangie . . . ?"

"Right beside you," Fargo told her.

Glory rolled her head so that she could look at her cousin. Vangie regained consciousness at that moment. She looked confused and disoriented for a few seconds, but finally she was able to say, "Glory? Skye?"

"Don't worry," Fargo said. "You're all right. It's over."

"The . . . the Apaches . . . ?"

"We're still their prisoners," Fargo replied honestly. As soon as the young women looked around, they would know that anyway. "I'm hoping Rafaelito will let us go now, though."

Glory said, "The last thing I remember, he was talking . . . some crazy story about Old Ones, and monsters, and curses . . ."

"I'll tell you all about it later," Fargo said. They might not like it when they found out he had agreed not to return to Skeleton Canyon, but the way Fargo saw it, that promise was a small price to pay for their lives.

Glory and Vangie dozed off, but it was a natural sleep this time and probably the best thing for them. Fargo was exhausted, too, but he stayed awake, still not completely trusting Rafaelito and the other Apaches. A while later, the women returned with

Fargo's buckskins and what was left of the clothes belonging to Glory and Vangie. Fargo thought it was a promising sign that their clothing was being returned to them.

Not his Colt and the Arkansas Toothpick, though. Evidently Rafaelito wasn't prepared to fully trust *him*, either.

Fargo pulled on the buckskins, grimacing a little as the clothes scraped over his blistered hide. Still, he felt better dressed. He let Glory and Vangie sleep, covering them with the blankets. He dozed a while himself, unable to fight off the weariness.

It was late in the afternoon when Rafaelito came into the hogan. By this time, Glory and Vangie had awakened and pulled on their tattered clothing.

"Tomorrow morning, you will leave and never come back," Rafaelito announced in Spanish. "If you do, you will be killed."

"What about our mounts?" Fargo asked.

"We have the mules ridden by the women and will return them," the war chief said. "That big black-and-white stallion of yours . . ." Rafaelito shook his head. "None of my men can catch him."

Fargo nodded. He wasn't surprised that the Apaches hadn't been able to lay hands on the Ovaro. The stallion would come when Fargo whistled for him, though.

"You will stay here tonight," Rafaelito went on. "Some of my warriors want to kill you, but I told them that you and I have given our word to each other, and Rafaelito honors his word."

"As do I," Fargo said.

Rafaelito nodded, apparently satisfied. "I will have food brought to you and your women." He rose and ducked out of the hogan.

Glory and Vangie seemed like they had been able to follow most of the conversation. Glory said in English, "Are we your women, Skye?"

"Rafaelito thinks so, anyway," Fargo replied.

"Probably wouldn't be a good idea to muddy the waters now."

"We don't intend to," Vangie said. "I think we'd probably be dead if it wasn't for you. We'll do whatever you say."

Glory nodded.

"Right now we'll just go along with what Rafaelito wants," Fargo said. "I'll bet Bert's mighty worried about you girls, back there in Gila City."

"Are you sure he's all right?" Vangie asked.

"He was fine when I rode out, just laid up with a bum knee."

The Apache women who had been there earlier came back with a pot of stew. Fargo didn't ask questions about what kind of meat was in the stew. He just spooned it out with his hands and ate heartily. Glory and Vangie were a bit reluctant at first, but their hunger got the best of them and soon they were eating just as eagerly as Fargo.

With full bellies, naturally they got drowsy again. The air cooled rapidly once the sun went down. There was only a tiny fire in the center of the hogan. The flames cast a feeble light and little heat. The three prisoners stretched out, rolling in the blankets and going to sleep.

Later in the night, Fargo came instantly awake as someone touched him softly. His eyes opened. The embers of the fire provided just enough illumination so that he could see Glory's long, fair hair as she knelt beside him. She touched his face again and then leaned over and kissed him.

Their lips parted and their tongues met. Fargo felt heat filling him, and although he knew some of that sensation was caused by the sunburn, he was confident that some of it was aroused by the sweet taste of Glory's mouth. She caught hold of his hand and lifted it, and he found his palm filled with the soft warmth of woman flesh. He had seen earlier that Glory's breasts weren't as large as Vangie's, and they were pear-shaped rather than globes, but Fargo didn't care. He stroked the hard nipple with his thumb.

When Glory lifted her lips from his, Fargo whispered, "What about Vangie?"

"She's asleep," Glory breathed against his ear. "Anyway, I wouldn't care if she wasn't. I heard the two of you, in camp a few nights ago. I figure it's my turn."

Fargo wasn't going to argue with her. What was that old saying, he asked himself, about turnabout being fair play . . . ?

"We'll have to be careful," Glory went on, so quietly that only Fargo could hear her. "We're both sunburned."

Only on their fronts, Fargo thought wryly. He didn't figure they could get very far, though, back to back.

Glory unfastened Fargo's buckskin trousers and pushed them down. She had already discarded the rags she had been wearing. She swung a leg over his hips and straddled him. She sat down first on his thighs so that his erection jutted up in front of her, and taking it in both hands she began gently stroking and caressing it. Fargo lay back and enjoyed her skilled touch. She leaned over and kissed the crown, then ran her tongue around the head. Several times she nearly brought him to a throbbing climax, but she always stopped just in time.

Finally neither of them could stand any more delay. Glory raised herself and brought the tip of Fargo's shaft to the honeyed opening between her legs. She lowered herself gradually, slowing engulfing the thick pole of male flesh inch by rock-hard inch. She gasped softly when at last she hit bottom.

Fargo lifted his hips, thrusting into her. She met his motion with a leisurely circling of her pelvis. It was a dance in slow motion, a sensuous pairing of man and woman, a timeless coming together. Fargo gave himself over to the sensations that coursed through him and let them wash away all the bad things that had happened today. The torture of the blazing sun was forgotten in the much sweeter heat of the climax that soon gripped them both . . .

And so, for a time, was the story of the Old Ones and the curse that lay on the gorge white men called Skeleton Canyon.

8

Fargo rode double with Glory on one of the mules when they left the Apache camp the next morning, after they had eaten and Fargo's weapons had been returned. All the warriors, around thirty of them, gathered to watch the white man and the two white women ride away. Rafaelito exchanged a solemn look with Fargo just before they left, and both men nodded in understanding. If they ever met again, it would probably be in a fight to the death.

The poultice of mud and roots and cactus juice had kept the sunburn from being too bad, but Fargo, Glory, and Vangie were all still blistered and sore this morning. It would be several days before they were back to normal. The tenderness wasn't so bad that it couldn't be tolerated, however. It was certainly outweighed by their relief at still being alive.

When they had gone perhaps half a mile from the camp, Fargo brought the mule to a halt and slid down from its back. He lifted his fingers to his mouth and gave a piercing whistle. Sure enough, a few moments later the Ovaro trotted into sight from behind some boulders, tossing his head in happiness as he came toward Fargo. Fargo greeted the stallion by rubbing his muzzle and then giving him an affectionate slap on the shoulder. The Ovaro nudged Fargo in return.

"How did you know he was close by?" Vangie asked.

"Well, every day is a new day for a horse," Fargo said, "but this big fella is smarter than most. He saw me being taken prisoner by the Apaches and knew something was wrong. He didn't let them catch him, but he stayed where I could call him when I needed him. He's done things like that before. A man couldn't ask for a better trail partner."

Fargo swung up into the saddle and took the lead. Having ridden over this part of the country the day before, he knew the way to the river.

"Are we really going back to Gila City?" Glory asked after a while.

"I gave Rafaelito my word," Fargo said. "Not to mention I promised your grandfather I'd get you two back safely."

"But what about all the gold?" Vangie said. "There's probably still a fortune in that canyon, Skye, and you know it!"

"Only one hombre ever died and came back from the grave, and gold didn't have a blessed thing to do with it," Fargo pointed out. "No amount of money is worth your life."

"Spoken like a man who's never been poor," Vangie said bitterly.

Fargo reined in and turned in the saddle to frown at them. "I've gone to sleep hungry more nights than you can count. I've been what some people would consider rich, and I've been stone broke more times than *I* can count. What I've learned from all that is that what matters are the people you know and the way you live your life. That's what adds up to a fortune, the way I see it."

The women didn't say anything, but after a moment Glory shrugged and heeled her mule into motion again. Vangie followed suit. Fargo took the point again, knowing that while they might not like abandoning the claim in Skeleton Canyon, they weren't going to argue about it anymore . . . at least not for a while.

Glory and Vangie had pulled their torn clothes together as best they could, but there was still a lot of skin showing through. And in the condition it was in, that skin was even more sensitive to the sun than usual. As the day grew hotter, Fargo called a halt every time he found some shade and let them cool off for a while. There was no rush to get back. He felt sure the Apaches were out there somewhere in this near-trackless wilderness, keeping an eye on them, but as long as he and the two women kept heading toward the river, they ought to be safe.

Of course, back in Gila City Bert Olmsted had to be mighty worried about his granddaughters, so Fargo didn't want to dawdle too much. The sooner they got back, the sooner the elderly Englishman's worries could be laid to rest.

They stopped in the shade of an overhanging bluff at midday and made a meager meal on jerky. There was a small pool of water under the bluff, formed there by an underground spring. Fargo refilled their canteens from the pool, and then Glory and Vangie unashamedly stripped off their clothes and splashed water on their sunburned skin, taking advantage of the opportunity to cool off. Fargo smiled as he watched them. They didn't seem to mind him looking, so he didn't feel guilty about getting an eyeful.

There was no telling where that interlude might have led if the sudden popping of distant gunshots hadn't come drifting through the hot, still air.

Fargo had been lounging with his hip propped against a small boulder. At the sound of trouble, he straightened quickly. Glory and Vangie had been dipping their tattered shirts in the pool and using the garments to splash water over themselves, but they stopped short and turned to look at Fargo. Glory asked, "Is that what I think it is?"

Fargo nodded. "Somebody's burning powder, all right. A rifle and a couple of pistols, I'd say."

"The Apaches?" Vangie said.

"No, the shooting's coming from the wrong direction," Fargo replied with a shake of his head. "The trouble's over closer to the river." He frowned. "Sounds to me like it's coming from the direction of the canyon."

"Skeleton Canyon, you mean?" Glory asked sharply.

"Yeah."

The girls started pulling on their wet clothing. "We have to go see what it's all about," Vangie declared.

Fargo shook his head again. "I gave Rafaelito my word we wouldn't go there."

"But if there's some sort of fight at the canyon, it's our business," Glory argued.

"Maybe it's Gramps!" Vangie exclaimed.

Fargo's frown deepened. As much as he hated to think about it, there was a possibility Vangie was right. Even with that wrenched knee, Bert Olmsted was capable of getting his hands on a horse and riding out of Gila City. He was hotheaded enough to do it, too. When Fargo hadn't returned that same night with Glory and Vangie, Olmsted might have decided to go back to Skeleton Canyon himself and look for them. He might have worried that something had happened to Fargo, causing the Trailsman not to catch up to the young women.

Those thoughts flashed through Fargo's mind. Despite the fact that he hated to break his word to Rafaelito, the chance that Olmsted might be in trouble meant that he had to investigate the shooting.

"Get dressed and ready to ride," he told Glory and Vangie. "We'll go take a look."

They were eager to get started and wasted no time pulling their clothes on. As they rode away from the pool, Fargo thought again about how the Apaches were probably watching them. They were asking for trouble by heading toward Skeleton Canyon, but Fargo didn't see any way to avoid it. They would just have to deal with that when the time came.

The shots sounded at a slower pace now, but they

105

hadn't stopped completely. From time to time there was a brief flurry of them, then another lull. Fargo cut across the rugged landscape, trying to take the shortest route to the canyon rather than returning to the river and following it.

The shooting stopped, but Fargo pressed on anyway, Glory and Vangie following him. When he thought they were only about half a mile from the canyon, a frantic burst of shots suddenly shattered the stillness, followed by several terrified screams. Fargo reined in as the shrieks died away to an ominous silence.

"My God," Glory said, her voice shaking a little. "What was that?"

"I never heard anything like it," Vangie said, sounding just as upset as her cousin.

Unfortunately, Fargo *had* heard sounds like that before. They were the screams of a man dying an agonizing death while in the grip of an unholy terror. But saying as much wouldn't do any good right now, so he heeled the Ovaro into motion again.

They approached the canyon from the top this time, rather than riding into it from below. This was where the Apaches had ambushed them and bombarded them with rocks. Fargo brought the stallion to a halt and dismounted, then motioned for Glory and Vangie to stay back. He slid the Henry from the saddle sheath, worked the lever to jack a cartridge into the chamber, and then walked toward the rim of the canyon.

When he looked down into it, the first things he saw were a couple of bedrolls lying on the ground about the same place where the tents had been set up earlier. Someone had come to the canyon and made camp there. If one of the bedrolls belonged to Olmsted, Fargo wondered who the old-timer had gotten to come with him.

He moved along the rim, peering down into the jumble of rocks that ran along the base of the canyon wall. The area was in the shade, but something caught

Fargo's eye anyway. It was a dark, reddish blotch on the ground, and when Fargo went down to one knee and squinted, he made out an irregular shape beside it.

His jaw tightened as he realized he was looking at a human body lying at the edge of a pool of blood.

"Skye?" Vangie called from where he had left them. "Skye, do you see anything?"

"Stay back," Fargo said.

"Skye, what is it?" Glory exclaimed worriedly.

Fargo took a deep breath. He couldn't lie to them. "There's a body down there."

"Oh, no!" That was Glory again.

Vangie asked grimly, "Is it Gramps?"

"I don't think so. The fella looks too big." There was something vaguely familiar about the dead man, Fargo thought, but he was going to have to get a closer look before he could recognize anybody.

Fargo stood again and moved farther along the rim toward the end of the canyon. He estimated that he was somewhere above the cave where he had found the skeleton chained to the wall. He walked on a little farther, then stopped abruptly as his guts went cold. The heat of the day was completely forgotten in the chill that gripped him.

He could see the place where they had buried the skeleton. The cairn of rocks they had erected over the grave had been disturbed. The rocks they had piled up were scattered all around now. Lying amidst those rocks was another body. The sun shone on this corpse, and in the light, the blood splashed everywhere was bright red.

That poor son of a bitch, whoever he had been, had met a truly grisly end. Something had chopped him to pieces.

This man was smaller than the first one Fargo had seen. The body might be Olmsted's, he thought. There was no question now that he had to go down and find out for sure. He turned, walked the other way until he came to the mouth of the canyon. He didn't see any other bodies, and no one was moving around down below.

When he got back to Glory and Vangie, he said, "I'm going to have to ride around until I can find a way down and get into the canyon."

"We know this country pretty well," Vangie said. "We can show you the way."

"What else did you see down there, Skye?" Glory asked. From the way both young women looked at him, Fargo knew they were not going to be put off. He was going to have to tell them.

"There's another body. It might be your grandfather. I can't be sure from up here."

They both paled under their sunburns. "Let's go," Vangie said tautly. "Follow us."

Fargo did. They wound around on a twisting trail that gradually led lower and lower until they came out on a flat stretch of ground leading to the canyon mouth. Fargo said, "I want you to stay out here while I ride in."

He expected them to argue, but they surprised him by agreeing. Both of them seemed a little stunned. Fargo supposed that was because they were worried about their grandfather. He didn't want them to see the gruesome remains of the man he feared might be Bert Olmsted.

With the Henry across the saddle in front of him, Fargo rode slowly into the canyon. The chill was still on him, and the shadows under the beetling walls didn't help matters. His eyes shuttled back and forth, alert for any threat. The canyon seemed to be empty, though, totally devoid of life.

He rounded the bend cautiously. He saw some boxes, probably used to carry supplies, scattered along the wall not far from the bedrolls and the first body. A pickax lay near the wall, too. Fargo frowned. He could understand Olmsted coming out here to look for his granddaughters, but why would the old-timer bring along supplies and mining equipment when he had abandoned the claim?

Fargo edged the stallion toward the rocks where the first body lay. Flies lifted from the bloody puddle in a buzzing cloud as he approached. Holding the rifle ready, Fargo kicked his feet out of the stirrups, swung his right leg over the stallion's back, and dropped to the ground.

Now that he was closer, he could see that this dead man had been torn up much like the other one. That was why so much blood had leaked out onto the ground. But the man's face was recognizable despite being slashed and contorted with terror and pain. His name was Luman, Fargo recalled, and he had been partnered with Mahaffey and Jessel, the men Bert Olmsted had regarded as potential claim jumpers.

It looked like Luman, at least, had jumped this claim . . . and it had cost him his life.

Remembering how the three men had tried to gun down him and Olmsted back in Gila City, Fargo didn't waste a lot of pity on Luman. Still, the man had been a human being, and Fargo didn't like to see anybody butchered this way. The only good thing about this discovery was that it meant it was less likely the other corpse was that of Bert Olmsted.

Fargo walked toward the end of the canyon. Again a horde of flies swarmed up protestingly as he drew near the second body. Not surprisingly, it belonged to Jessel.

For a long moment, Fargo stood there, solemnly regarding the blood-drenched corpse. He scraped a thumbnail along his jawline with its close-cropped beard as he frowned in thought. As he studied the scattered rocks that had formed the cairn, the conclusion he drew was inescapable. Luman and Jessel—and maybe Mahaffey, too, for that matter, although there was no sign of him—had thrown the rocks aside. Had they been planning to dig into the grave and see who was buried there?

Was anybody still buried there? When Fargo looked closer, he saw that the dirt already had been disturbed. Had the claim jumpers dug into it?

Or, once the rocks had been removed, had something dug its way *out*?

"That's crazy," Fargo muttered aloud. He had always been a hard-headed, practical man, not given to moments of such grotesque whimsy. That yarn Rafaelito had spun about the Old Ones, and curses and monsters, must have addled him a mite, he told himself. Dead was dead, and nothing could put flesh back on naked bones and animate it.

But someone or something had killed Luman and Jessel and done it in a particularly nasty fashion, too.

The floor of the canyon was sandy enough to hold tracks. Fargo saw a lot of boot prints as he looked around. His eyes narrowed as he saw something else: bare footprints. Big ones, too, that had been made by a heavy, powerful man.

Or a monster who wore the skin of a man . . .

"Damn it," Fargo growled. He needed to quit thinking about things like that. It was difficult to do, though, like when a fella had bet him in a saloon that he couldn't go a full minute without thinking about an elephant. Fargo had given up on that one before he lost another dollar.

Though turning his back on Jessel's body and the desecrated grave made the back of his neck crawl a little, he swung around and hurried along the canyon to the spot where he had left the Ovaro. He caught up the reins and led the stallion to the bend. Now that he knew Olmsted wasn't here and evidently hadn't been here, he and Glory and Vangie needed to light a shuck away from the canyon. If they got back to the river trail and rode hard toward Gila City, there was a slim chance the Apaches might let them go unmolested.

One thing was certain, he thought. The Apaches couldn't be blamed for the deaths of Luman and Jessel. Rafaelito and his warriors wouldn't set foot in the canyon. Somebody else had jumped the claim jumpers. Luman and Jessel had put up a fight; Fargo knew that because he had heard the shooting. In the end, though, their guns hadn't saved them.

Where was Mahaffey? It was possible he hadn't been here when the attack took place. Or he might have been taken prisoner and carried off by whoever had killed his partners. Fargo didn't know and at this point didn't really care. He just wanted to get Glory and Vangie and hit the trail for Gila City as fast as he could.

They were waiting for him right at the mouth of the canyon, their faces tight with worry. Fargo swung up into the saddle and rode to meet them. Right away, to put their minds at ease, he said, "Olmsted's not in there. I imagine he's back in Gila City, resting that bum knee."

"Thank God," Glory said.

Vangie asked, "What about the dead man you saw? Who was it?"

"There were two of them . . . Jessel and Luman."

The women stared at him for a second, digesting that news, and then Vangie exclaimed angrily, "Those bastards jumped the claim, just like we thought they would!"

"They didn't waste any time about it, either," Glory said. "As soon as they found out we were gone, they moved right in."

"And it was a bad move for them, the way it turned out," Fargo said.

"What about Mahaffey?"

Fargo shook his head. "No sign of him. I don't know if he's dead or alive, and I don't care. Let's get moving. Maybe we can get away from here before Rafaelito comes after us for breaking our word."

They wheeled their mounts and were about to start toward the river when a rifle blasted somewhere nearby. Fargo heard the flat *whap!* of the bullet as it ripped through the air beside his ear. More shots roared out. Slugs kicked up dust around the feet of the suddenly skittish horses.

"Come on!" Fargo shouted as he whirled the Ovaro toward the canyon mouth. Going back in that charnel house was about the last thing on earth he wanted to do, but it beat sitting out in the open while they were being bushwhacked.

With Glory and Vangie riding hard behind him, Fargo galloped into the canyon. Bullets whined past them and pocked the sandstone walls. When Fargo reached a cluster of boulders, he dropped from the saddle with the Henry in his left hand and sent the stallion racing on around the bend with a swat on the horse's rump. The women dismounted on the run as well. Fargo hustled them behind the rocks and told them to get down. He didn't have to repeat the order. They dropped to their bellies on the sandy ground.

Fargo knelt behind one of the boulders and lined the barrel of the rifle on the canyon mouth. Outside on the flat, he saw a brown figure dart from one rock to another, moving closer to the canyon. He bit back a curse. He and Vangie and Glory had been too slow getting away from here. The Apaches had caught up to them. And as it had turned out, there hadn't been any reason for them to come here. Bert Olmsted had not returned to Skeleton Canyon.

Now they were pinned down, and it was probably only a matter of time until the Apaches picked them off, either from outside the canyon or from the rim above. The only thing Fargo was relatively sure of was that Rafaelito and his men wouldn't enter the canyon itself to come after them.

"Skye, what are we going to do?" Vangie asked.

"Maybe we could talk to Rafaelito," Glory suggested.

Fargo shook his head grimly. "We've already broken our word to him once. He wouldn't believe us again, no matter what we promised him."

"Then maybe we could make a run for it," Vangie said.

It might come down to that, Fargo thought, but if it did, it would be largely a futile gesture, a final act of defiance. A foolhardy play like that was almost the same thing as giving up, because the result would be the same—death for all three of them.

"We'll try waiting them out," he said. "They're already not shooting as much as they were before."

That was true. The shots had died away and sounded only sporadically now. The three people trapped in the canyon were behind good cover, and it would take a lucky shot or a ricochet to hit them. Such a thing wasn't out of the question, of course, but just blazing away indiscriminately at the canyon mouth would be a waste of powder and lead. The Apaches couldn't afford that.

"Keep an eye on the rim," Fargo told Glory and Vangie. "Sing out if you see anybody moving around up there. I'll watch the mouth of the canyon."

"They won't come in to get us," Vangie said.

"I know it, but Rafaelito might have something else up his sleeve."

As the sun moved farther west in the sky, the heat in the canyon grew worse. After enduring the torment the Apaches had put them through, Fargo and his two companions knew they could stand a little heat. Every so often one of the warriors fired a shot into the canyon mouth, but most of the time the place was quiet, so quiet that after a while the silence was enough to get on a fella's nerves, Fargo thought.

As the sun lowered still more, late in the afternoon, it reflected off something half-buried in the sand near the rock where Fargo waited. He ignored the reflection at first, but finally his curiosity grew too great. He couldn't reach whatever it was without exposing himself to the fire of the Apaches, but he was able to extend the barrel of the Henry, hook it in what seemed to be a loop of metal, and jerk the thing toward him.

Even that was enough to draw the fire of one of the warriors. A rifle barked outside the canyon, and a split second later the bullet spanged off the boulder Fargo was using as cover. He hunkered lower and used the rifle barrel to drag the thing he had unearthed over to him.

He recognized it right away, and the sight sent a shiver up his spine. It was a metal ring, a shackle attached to a bit of chain only a few inches long. The last time Fargo had seen it, it had been around the bony wrist of the skeleton in the cave.

He might have thought that it was a different shackle, except that he recognized the piece of chain. He had used the chisel to separate it from the rest of the chain. As he picked up the shackle, he saw the same symbols carved into the dull, age-pitted iron. He ran a fingertip over them and felt an odd tingle.

That was nerves again, he told himself. But he had every right to be nervous, considering the fact that this shackle had been on the skeleton, and the skeleton was supposed to be in that grave at the other end of the canyon. How had the shackle gotten all the way over here?

The answer was simple, Fargo thought as his eyes narrowed. *Somebody had put the shackle here.* More than likely the same somebody who had killed Luman and Jessel in such a gruesome manner. And whoever had done that had probably dug up the grave, too. As for the reason . . .

It all came back to the gold.

The Apaches considered this canyon cursed and wouldn't enter it. Maybe the killer, or killers, wanted everybody else to steer clear of it, too. Skeleton Canyon already had a bad name. If word got around that the skeleton in question had climbed up out of its grave and butchered two men in bloody fashion, nobody would want anything to do with the place, no matter how strong the lure of the riches that might be found here.

The theory made sense, Fargo decided as he mulled it over. But that was all it was, a theory. He hadn't been here when Luman and Jessel died, and he had no proof about any of it. He thought it odd that Mahaffey wasn't here, though. Maybe the third claim jumper hadn't been in on the plan. . . .

"What's that you've got, Skye?" Vangie suddenly asked.

Fargo glanced down at the shackle in his hand and then slid it inside his buckskin shirt. "Nothing important," he said. Vangie and Glory had enough to worry about right now, what with being trapped in here by the Apaches and all.

The Apaches hadn't given up and gone away, either. Fargo hadn't really believed they would, but he had held on to that hope anyway. A short time later, he saw how desperate their situation really was, as some of the warriors, hidden behind the cliffs on either side of the canyon mouth, began tossing bundles of dried brush into the opening. Fargo would have tried to pick them off, but he never got a good shot at them.

"What are they doing?" Glory asked.

"One of the things I was worried about," Fargo said. His expression was bleak. "They're going to try to smoke us out."

9

The Apaches continued building a wall of brush across the mouth of the canyon. They used what was already there to conceal their movements as they crawled out with more bundles. Fargo gritted his teeth in frustration as he watched. He could put a few rounds through the brush, but he would be firing blind, with no way of knowing if he had hit any of the warriors. Even if he did, he doubted that it would stop them.

"They're going to set that brush on fire?" Vangie asked.

Fargo nodded. "That's what I figure."

"But the fire won't get this far."

"The smoke will." Fargo wet a finger in his mouth and stuck it in the air. There wasn't much breeze in the canyon, but what there was of it was moving in a swirling pattern, into the canyon and then back out of it.

That was why the first smoke he smelled came from the far end of the canyon, not the brush pile at the mouth.

He heard the horses whinnying shrilly, back around the bend. Glory looked around, wide-eyed, and asked, "What's going on?"

"Some of the other Indians are setting fire to bundles of brush and dropping them into the canyon behind us," Fargo explained. "The way the wind's moving, it'll carry the smoke right to us. The smoke from the canyon mouth will come the other way, once they fire that brush, and we'll be caught in the middle. The air in here won't be fit to breathe after a while."

"What do we do then?" Vangie asked tautly.

"Either choke to death, or come out of the canyon."

"And then they'll kill us," Glory said. It wasn't a question.

"That's the idea, anyway."

"What else can we do?" Vangie said.

Fargo didn't know, but he wasn't going to give up yet. His brain worked furiously.

Flames shot up in the gathering dusk as the Apaches lit the brush barrier across the mouth of the canyon. Clouds of smoke billowed from it and rolled ponderously toward Fargo and the women. The choking stuff began to edge around the bend from the other direction, too, driving the animals in front of it. The Ovaro was keeping his head, as usual, but the two mules were panic-stricken. They bolted suddenly, galloping toward the canyon mouth.

The Apaches had left a gap in the barrier. They wanted the whites to come out, so that they could be killed outside the canyon. Given the Apaches' fear of the place, if Fargo, Glory, and Vangie died while inside the canyon, the warriors would never be able to come in and make sure they were dead. They would just have to assume as much. And Rafaelito clearly wanted to be sure.

So the terrified mules had some place to flee. They raced past before Fargo had any chance to try to stop them and headed straight for the gap. They galloped through the opening. Rifles blasted as the Apaches opened fire before waiting to see if the mules had riders. The shooting stopped quickly. Fargo didn't know if the mules had been killed or not. He couldn't see well enough through the thick smoke.

The Ovaro stopped next to Fargo. The stallion tossed his head and whickered, clearly worried and upset by the stinging, blinding smoke. He wanted

Fargo to climb on and get out of here. Fargo knew that he couldn't. This was one time the Ovaro had to go on without him.

If he couldn't see the Apaches to shoot at them, they couldn't draw a bead on him, either. He stood up and went to the stallion. He stroked the horse's neck and said quietly, "You've got to go, big fella. I'll see you later, if I can."

The horse nuzzled Fargo's shoulder. The bond between man and horse was a tough one to break, especially when they had been through as much together as these two had. Fargo caught hold of the reins, turned the Ovaro toward the canyon mouth, and said sharply, "Go!" He yanked off his hat and slapped it against the stallion's rump to reinforce the command.

The stallion might not have liked it, but he did as he was told. He lunged forward in a run, heading for the gap in the blazing barrier. Fargo knew he was sending his old friend into danger, but the stallion had a better chance this way. The Apaches would have a hard time hitting such a swift target. Fargo's eyes stung from the smoke as he lost sight of the Ovaro in the billowing clouds.

He heard the roar of guns, though, and uttered a silent prayer that the stallion would make it through all right.

He had done all he could for the Ovaro. Now he had to try to save his life, and the lives of Glory and Vangie. He had the glimmering of an idea, and the more he thought about it, the stronger the possibility seemed to be.

"Come on," he said to the women. "They can't see us anymore."

Glory coughed from the smoke and then asked, "Where are we going?"

"Deeper into the canyon," Fargo said. He took Glory's hand. "Hang on to Vangie."

The three of them held on to each other so they wouldn't be separated as they worked their way along the canyon wall toward the bend. When they went around it, Fargo saw the burning mounds of brush that had been thrown into the canyon back here. The smoke was even thicker around the bend. He looked up and couldn't see the rims at all.

That was good. It meant the Apaches still couldn't see them.

He felt along the wall with the hand holding the rifle until he came to what he was looking for. The narrow ledge that led to the cave climbed the wall to his left. "Follow me," he said to Glory and Vangie. "You'll have to step up onto the ledge."

"Won't the smoke . . . be even worse . . . higher up?" Vangie choked out. Both girls were coughing hard now.

Fargo's eyes streamed and his nose and throat burned. It seemed like he would never take a breath of clean, cool air again. But they had to push on. Their only chance lay above them, at the end of the ledge.

"Just climb!" he told them.

The harrowing, smoke-choked ascent reminded Fargo of the first time he had climbed the ledge. He hadn't been able to see much then, either. But at least he had been able to breathe. Now every gasping breath was torture. He shuffled along, inch by inch, feeling his way with his feet and the hand holding the rifle. His other hand hung on tight to Glory, and he hoped she was gripping Vangie's hand just as tightly.

Finally, after what seemed like an eternity, Fargo felt the opening to his left that marked the mouth of the cave. "We're here," he announced to the girls. "Watch your heads as you go in."

Glory pulled back. "In . . . in that cave?"

"Where the skeleton was?" Vangie added.

Fargo didn't take the time to explain. He just tugged them after him as he growled, "Let's go."

The air was noticeably better as soon as he moved into the cave. Some smoke had drifted in, but it wasn't nearly as thick here. The flow of air through the tiny holes in the back of the cave was strong enough to keep most of the smoke out. The siren song he had heard on his first visit to this cave was now going to save their lives. The Apaches never came into the canyon. None of them had set foot in the cave since their medicine men had captured the sole surviving Old One and chained him to the wall, however many years—or centuries—ago that had been. They wouldn't know that there was fresh air in the cave.

It was pitch-black inside, even though outside it was still twilight. Fargo fumbled his way toward the rear of the cave, leading Glory and Vangie. He ran into the back wall and pressed his face against it. He felt coolness, took a deep breath and smelled clean air, free of the taint of smoke.

"Up here," Fargo grated through his raw throat. "There's good air here."

Glory and Vangie crowded up against the wall next to him and eagerly breathed the fresher air. Fargo leaned against the sandstone in exhaustion, even his muscular body and iron constitution drained by the events of the past few days. Slowly, first Glory and then Vangie slipped to the floor of the cave. The air was still good enough there, although it was a bit more smoky. Fargo slid down and joined them.

He turned so that his back was against the cave wall and pointed the Henry at the opening. He had fifteen rounds in the rifle, as well as five in the Colt's cylinder and some extra cartridges in the loops on his belt. If anybody came into the cave, they would get a hot lead reception. Fargo didn't really think that was very likely, though. The Apaches would be too frightened to come check on them.

Glory was to his right, Vangie to his left. They slumped against him as they dozed off. Fargo was drowsy, too, but he managed to stay awake. The cave stunk, and he realized after a while that it smelled of more than smoke. The musty odor that had been here during his first visit still lingered, even though the skeleton was gone. It still smelled somehow like death.

But the cave represented life to Fargo and the two women. They would stay here all night if necessary, waiting for the Apaches to leave.

Sometime during the night, Fargo must have dozed off without meaning to, because he had a dream. In the dream someone came into the cave and walked toward him. Someone or some*thing*. It moved in a shambling walk, sort of like a man but not really. Fargo looked at it and felt his skin crawl and his heart seemed to jump up in his throat. He wanted to yell, not in fear, exactly, but more in outrage that something like this could even exist on God's green earth. The intruder leaned down and reached for him. Fargo's brain commanded him to jerk the trigger on the Henry and blast a hole in the son of a bitch's guts, but his muscles all seemed frozen. He couldn't move, couldn't fight, and that was the worst feeling of all.

Then the hand that wasn't a hand pulled back, and the thing flinched away from him, backing toward the cave mouth as if it were frightened. It loomed there for a second, bulky and misshapen in silhouette against the faint starlight, and then was gone.

Sunlight was splashing brilliantly into the cave as Fargo came awake with a sharply indrawn breath. All the smoke was gone. He lifted the Henry, but there was nothing to shoot at. His pulse hammered in his head. Slowly, he began to realize that the unearthly visitor had been nothing but a dream. His racing pulse eased.

This place was enough to give anybody the fantods, even a fella who had been to see the elephant a time or two.

Glory and Vangie began to stir on either side of him. Vangie opened her mouth to say something, but Fargo laid a finger on her lips to silence her. He had just heard something . . . a footstep, he thought.

A harsh voice called out. Fargo recognized the words as Apache. Another warrior who was farther away shouted something in return. Several more chimed in.

Glory and Vangie stared at Fargo in confusion. He could follow enough of the conversation to know that the Apaches were moving along the rims of the canyon, looking down into it, searching for the bodies of Fargo and the two women.

He whispered as much to Glory and Vangie, adding, "They can't find us, but they're pretty sure we're dead. They think we choked to death on the smoke."

"They know about this cave," Vangie whispered. "Won't they think we hid in it?"

"That might not occur to them. Even if it did, they won't come into the canyon to check."

They fell silent then, not wanting their voices to filter up through the holes in the cliff. If Rafaelito knew they were still alive, the war chief would squat outside the canyon until doomsday if he had to, waiting for them to come out so that he could kill them. But if he believed they were dead, sooner or later the Apaches would leave. They might keep a watch on the place for a while, though, so Fargo and the two women would have to be patient.

The voices called back and forth for a while and then faded as the Apaches moved away. That didn't mean they were gone, though. Fargo warned Glory and Vangie that they would have to wait and be as quiet as possible while they were doing it.

Fargo's eyes were drawn to the dust on the floor. It was too smudged and disturbed to tell if there were any fresh footprints in it. Anyway, he told himself, that eerie visitation had been a dream, that was all. He wasn't going to find any evidence because it hadn't really happened.

After a time he stood up and moved quietly toward the cave mouth. He stayed far enough back so that he couldn't be seen by anyone standing on the opposite rim. He listened intently, his keen ears searching for any telltale noises that would reveal the continued presence of the Apaches near the canyon. He didn't hear anything except the sighing of the wind.

Fargo wasn't ready to believe that Rafaelito and the other warriors were gone. He went back to join Glory and Vangie near the rear wall. He sat down and whispered, "We'll wait longer."

Despite the sleep they had gotten during the night, the two women were still exhausted. Fargo could see the weariness in the tight-drawn lines of their faces. He figured he looked about the same way. But rushing things now could get them killed, so it was better to wait.

Time dragged by. The shifting of the sunlight told Fargo that hours had passed. Several times he had ventured up near the mouth of the cave to listen. The canyon and the surrounding vicinity were still quiet.

Then, sometime during the afternoon, the clopping of hoofbeats sounded from the canyon. The sandy canyon floor muffled them somewhat, but Fargo had no trouble hearing them. A moment later, a horse neighed, and it might as well have been the voice of an old friend calling out to Fargo.

The Ovaro!

If the big black-and-white stallion had come back into the canyon, that could mean only one thing. The Apaches had left, and now the Ovaro was searching for the Trailsman. Fargo didn't know whether he was more relieved that the Apaches were gone or that the stallion had survived the shooting the night before. Both those bits of news were more than welcome.

He came to his feet and said, "We can leave now. That's my stallion out there."

"You think the Apaches are finally gone?" Glory asked.

"I know they are. That big fella wouldn't have come into the canyon if they weren't."

Fargo helped the women stand up. Their muscles

were stiff and sore. He led them to the mouth of the cave, and they paused there to look out at the canyon. The edges of it were in shadow, as usual, but the sun shone brightly in the middle, and that was where the Ovaro stood, tossing his head. Fargo whistled, and the stallion's head-tossing became more emphatic.

Vangie laughed. "He's waving to you," she said.

"I reckon you're probably right," Fargo agreed. "Take it easy going down that ledge. After all we've been through, we don't want to slip and fall now."

He went first, moving carefully. Behind him, one of the women gasped, and he knew she must have gotten a look at Jessel's mutilated body. They hadn't seen either of the corpses until now.

"Don't look any more than you have to," Fargo told them. "It's not a pretty sight, and neither is Luman's body."

"Skye . . ." Vangie said. "It looks like somebody's been messing with that grave. All the rocks are thrown aside, and somebody's been . . . digging . . ."

"I know."

"But why would anybody do such an awful thing?" Glory asked.

"I've got an idea," Fargo said. As they continued to descend the ledge, he explained his theory about someone killing Jessel and Luman to make the prospect of looking for gold in Skeleton Canyon even less appealing.

"You mean they were killed just to scare off everybody else?" Vangie asked. Clearly, she was having a hard time believing it.

"That's terrible!" Glory added.

Fargo had reached the bottom of the ledge. He hopped off and turned to help them step down to the canyon floor. "Some men will do just about anything for gold," he said. "A lot of fellas have been murdered for the sake of it before now."

"I suppose you're right," Glory said. A shudder ran through her. "Still, to do a thing like that . . ."

"Who do you think was responsible for it?" Vangie asked. "What happened to Mahaffey? He's not here, is he?"

"I didn't see his body anywhere, and I checked the whole canyon," Fargo replied. "He might have double-crossed the other two."

"Since they were partners, they probably trusted him," Vangie said. "He could have snuck up on them . . . but where is he now?"

Fargo shook his head. "I don't know. Don't really care. I just want to get you girls back to Gila City."

"What about . . . them?" Glory asked. "Do we bury them?"

"No time. I'm sorry, but we'll just have to leave them."

"I'm not sorry," Vangie said. "They would have killed us and stolen our claim if they thought they could get away with it."

Fargo nodded and said, "There's that to consider, too."

The stallion had trotted over to him, whickering happily at being reunited. Fargo took the reins and led the horse toward the mouth of the canyon. Glory and Vangie trudged along behind them. When they reached the entrance, Fargo stopped to look around, holding the Henry ready for instant use if he needed it. He didn't see any signs of impending trouble, though. The Apaches really were gone.

The two mules Glory and Vangie had been riding were nowhere in sight. If the Apaches had killed them when they charged out of the canyon, fleeing the fire and smoke, the bodies would be here, or at least part of them. Apaches did have a fondness for mule meat. The fact that they were gone told Fargo they had escaped. But either way, there were three humans and only one horse.

"You two climb on," he told Glory and Vangie. "The stallion can carry double, especially when the riders are light, like you."

"What about you, Skye?" Glory asked.

"I'll walk. It won't be the first time."

"Gila City is too far away. You can't walk all that way."

"Sure I can. We just won't make very good time, that's all."

"We can take turns," Vangie suggested. "You can ride part of the time, too."

"We'll see," Fargo said. "For now, climb on up there and let's get moving."

The women complied. Vangie stepped up into the saddle, and Glory climbed on behind and held her cousin around the waist. Fargo gave Vangie the reins and then set out on the trail that led west to the Colorado River.

They moved alone through the vast landscape and might as well have been the only human beings in a thousand miles. Fargo knew that wasn't true, of course. And the loneliness didn't bother him, since any man who spent much time on the frontier quickly grew accustomed to solitude or else went mad. It was the middle of the day. Fargo knew that at this pace, they wouldn't make it back to Gila City until sometime the next day, at the earliest.

Later in the afternoon, though, after they had reached the river and turned south, fortune finally smiled on them. Fargo held up a hand to call a halt as he spotted the two mules up ahead, grazing on spotty clumps of tough grass.

"Stay here," he told Glory and Vangie. "I'll see if I can catch them."

He left the rifle with the girls and slowly walked forward. When the mules raised their heads and looked warily at him, he began to talk to them in soft, comforting tones. What he said didn't matter; it was the way he said it. The mules blew through their noses and took a few nervous steps, but they didn't turn and run. Fargo continued his gradual approach until he was close enough to reach out and take hold of one set of reins. Still moving slowly, he caught the other set as well.

Once Fargo had hold of the reins, he led the mules back to where Glory and Vangie waited on the Ovaro.

"Here you go," he said to them as they dismounted. "We'll be able to move along faster now."

With all three of them mounted again, Fargo set a swifter pace. He was anxious to get the women back to Gila City where they would be safe. Out here in the wilderness, there were too many things that could happen, too many dangers that could crop up without warning.

They stayed on the trail for long hours, gnawing on jerky from Fargo's saddlebags to ease their hunger, washing down the tough strips of dried meat with water from the canteen. Fargo called an occasional halt to rest the animals, but they were few and far between. After a brief twilight, night fell with its usual suddenness, but Fargo didn't stop. They slowed down but pushed on, following the trail by starlight. When the moon rose, they were able to move faster again.

It was far into the night by the time they reached the spot where the Gila flowed into the Colorado from the east. The ferrymen's cabin was dark. Fargo rode past it with Glory and Vangie trailing him. When he glanced back, he saw that both of them were swaying a little, worn out from the long ride on top of everything else that had happened. But it was only a few more miles to Gila City, and he thought they could make it that far.

A short time later, Fargo slowed as he reached the outskirts of the settlement. Glory and Vangie rode up beside him. "My God," Vangie muttered. "We made it."

"I want to fall in bed and sleep for a week," Glory said. "And when I get up, I want to spend another week soaking in a nice hot bath."

Vangie practically moaned. "That sounds wonderful!"

Fargo grinned in the darkness. "Mind if I join you?" he asked.

Vangie reached over and put a hand on his arm. "In bed or in the bath? Either way doesn't sound bad at all."

Glory touched his shoulder and added, "No, it sure doesn't."

"Well, I reckon the first thing we need to do is find your grandfather and let him know you two are all right. I'll bet that old-timer is about out of his head with worry by now."

"You're probably right about that," Glory said. "You think he missed us, Vangie?"

She laughed. "I'm sure he did."

Fargo thought there was something a little odd about the way they sounded, but he was too tired to puzzle it out at the moment. He headed for the hotel. Most of the buildings in Gila City were dark, since it was the middle of the night. A lamp burned in the lobby of the hotel, though. And of course the Pine Tree Saloon was still lit up, since it never really closed. The faint sounds of talk and laughter drifted past the batwings.

Fargo intended to find out if Mahaffey had turned up in Gila City following the gruesome deaths of his partners Luman and Jessel. But again, that could wait until after he had reunited Bert Olmsted with the old man's granddaughters. Fargo reined up in front of the hotel and swung down from the saddle. He looped the Ovaro's reins over the hitch rail while Glory and Vangie were dismounting.

The clerk behind the desk in the hotel lobby was dozing as the three of them came in. He muttered, shook his head, then lifted it and opened his eyes. They kept opening until he was staring at them.

"Mr. Fargo!" he exclaimed. "And Miss Glory and Miss Vangie! You're alive!"

"Why shouldn't we be?" Fargo asked. They had come within a whisker of death many times during the past few days, but the clerk had no way of knowing that.

Or maybe he did, Fargo thought.

That guess was confirmed a second later when the man said, "Jack Mahaffey said the Apaches killed all three of you."

"Been telling that tale all over town, has he?"

"Yeah. Not as much as the one about the monster, of course—"

Fargo held up a hand to stop him. "The monster?" he repeated.

The clerk nodded eagerly. "That's right. The Monster of Skeleton Canyon, folks are calling it. The thing that killed Luman and Jessel. Tore them up something fierce, to hear Mahaffey tell it." The man shuddered. "I'll tell you what, there's not enough gold in the world to make me want to go up to that place."

And that was exactly how Mahaffey wanted everyone to feel, Fargo thought. He exchanged a glance with Glory and Vangie and saw that they realized his theory had been right, too.

That could wait. Fargo jerked a thumb toward the second floor and asked, "Bert Olmsted still up there in the same room?"

"Yes, sir. He's getting around a lot better now."

"Thanks." Fargo gestured toward the stairs and said to Glory and Vangie, "Come on."

He ushered them upstairs and down the hall to Olmsted's room. A knock on the door prompted a sleepy, "Huh? Whazzit?" from inside. Fargo tried the knob, found it unlocked, and opened the door. As he stepped in, Olmsted was sitting up in bed, lighting a lamp and pointing a pistol toward the door.

"Take it easy, old-timer," the Trailsman told him. "It's me, Fargo, and I've got Glory and Vangie with me."

"Lord bless me!" Olmsted exclaimed as he gaped at them. He put the pistol on the table beside the bed and sprang up, his long nightshirt flapping around his spindly calves. He rushed over to them, threw his arms around Glory, and planted a hard, passionate kiss directly on her mouth.

Then, while Fargo was looking startled and thinking that wasn't a very grandfatherly way to behave, Olmsted grabbed Vangie and did the same thing to her.

10

"Wait just a damned minute," Fargo said, unable to suppress his consternation. "What's going on here?"

Olmsted suddenly let go of Vangie and stepped back, putting a little distance between them. He looked completely flustered as he said, "I, ah, I'm simply, ah, overjoyed to see my, ah, granddaughters. That's all."

Glory laughed and said, "You might as well give up, Gramps."

"That's right," Vangie said. "After the way Skye just saw you shove your tongue halfway down our throats, I think he's probably figured out that you're not really our grandfather."

"I most certainly am!" Olmsted insisted. "You call me Gramps, don't you?"

"You can call the sun the moon, but that doesn't make it so," Fargo said. His eyes narrowed in suspicion. "I still want to know what's going on here. Who are you people?"

"Just who we said we are," Vangie replied, "except for the fact that he's not our grandfather. We just started calling him Gramps because he's such a dear old scalawag, and that gave him the idea to pretend that we're related. He thought men might be more likely to leave us alone if they thought our grandfather was looking out for us."

Fargo looked from her to Glory and back again. "Are the two of you even cousins?"

"As a matter of fact, we are," Glory said. "And we really grew up in New Mexico Territory, just like we told you, Skye."

"We worked at a place in Santa Fe," Vangie added. "That's where Gramps met us."

"A place?" Fargo repeated.

"Well . . ." Glory said, and surprisingly, both young women blushed. "A whorehouse, I guess you'd say."

"We're soiled doves," Vangie said.

"We *were* soiled doves," Glory said. "We've given it up, though."

"We partnered with Gramps and came over here to look for gold and find our fortunes."

Fargo looked at Olmsted. "And you let them come along?"

The old-timer spread his hands. "Look at 'em, lad, just look at 'em! What man would turn down such an offer, even a decrepit old bag of bones like me!"

Fargo was angry at being deceived, but at the same time, he could see Olmsted's point. Glory and Vangie were lovely, and they had also proven that they were courageous and didn't mind hard work. They would make good partners for a man, if he didn't mind taking women into a situation that could be dangerous. Clearly, Olmsted had thought that having their help was worth the risk.

Glory touched Fargo's arm. "Skye, you forgive us for lying to you, don't you? It didn't really make any difference in what happened."

"No, I suppose it didn't," Fargo admitted.

"And we were going to tell you when we got back," Vangie said. "We already talked about it and agreed you had a right to know. We just didn't figure on Gramps getting so carried away when he saw us."

"A man gets urges—" Olmsted began defensively.

Fargo held up a hand to stop him. "No need to go into that. I reckon it's best to just leave things as they are. Glory's right, it really doesn't make a lot of difference to me whether you're related or not."

Olmsted took the girls' hands and sat down on the edge of the bed with them. "Tell me everything that happened," he said. "I've been goin' out of my mind with worry."

Glory and Vangie hesitated, but then, taking turns, they explained how they had been unwilling to give up the claim in Skeleton Canyon. They told Olmsted how they had been captured by Rafaelito and the other Apaches as they were trying to return to the diggings.

"But then Skye came along and saved us," Glory said.

Fargo snorted in self-deprecation. "Didn't do a very good job of it. I wound up a prisoner just like the two of you."

"But you got those savages to let us go," Vangie said. "And then you really did save our lives in the canyon."

Olmsted looked confused and said, "I thought you never got there."

"There's more to the story," Glory said. She told the old-timer about being trapped in the canyon by the Apaches.

"You're all bloody lucky to be alive," Olmsted said. "If the Apaches didn't get you, the monster should have."

"The monster that Mahaffey's talking about around town?" Fargo looked grim. "No monster killed Luman and Jessel. A man did that."

"How can you be sure?" Olmsted asked. "From the sound of what you told me about Rafaelito's story, that thing must have been the Old One. It came out of that grave where we put the skeleton and killed those two poor bastards."

Glory and Vangie stared at Fargo. "Do you think that could be true, Skye?" Vangie asked.

"The grave had definitely been disturbed," Glory added worriedly.

"Either Mahaffey killed them, or he's working with the men who did," Fargo said. "I intend to find out which."

"Then there's no monster?"

For a second, Fargo's brain flashed back to that strange dream and the misshapen figure that had played such a large part in it. But then he shook his head and said, "I don't think so. Unless you want to count the monster that greed makes out of men."

Fargo left Glory and Vangie at the hotel with Olmsted. He had a hard time not thinking of the old man as their grandfather, and he was still a little angry at the deception. But right now, after the hardships of the past few days, he was more interested in getting a drink and then some sleep. He walked toward the Pine Tree.

It seemed like more than a month had passed since he first rode into Gila City and into the middle of the trouble between Olmsted and Flynn Pearsoll, instead of a week or so. A lot had happened during that time. He had dodged the reaper's scythe more than once, and he had seen men die ugly deaths. He wasn't sure what he was going to do about Mahaffey. The idea that the man might get away with murder offended Fargo's sense of justice, but he wasn't a lawman. He couldn't just go up to Mahaffey and arrest him for killing Luman and Jessel. Besides, Fargo reflected, he still didn't know for sure that Mahaffey was responsible for their deaths, even though the fact that Mahaffey was spreading stories about a monster in Skeleton Canyon told Fargo the man was guilty.

Either that, or there really was a monster . . .

He smiled to himself as that thought crossed his mind. He needed that drink more than he had thought.

He wasn't going to get it right away, though, because before he could reach the saloon, a familiar figure pushed through the batwings. Fargo recognized the tall, brawny shape of Flynn Pearsoll.

Normally, Fargo would have marched right up to Pearsoll without a second thought. He wasn't in the habit of stepping aside from possible trouble. But another man emerged from the Pine Tree and fell in step beside Pearsoll, and as Fargo recognized that man he stepped into the dark mouth of the alley next to the assay office to wait and see where they were going.

The second man was Jack Mahaffey. As far as Fargo knew, there was no connection between Pearsoll and Mahaffey. They seemed friendly enough, though, and were talking together in low tones as they moved along the boardwalk toward the alley where Fargo waited in the shadows. Pearsoll didn't have his usual crew of gunnies with him tonight, but that didn't mean they weren't close-by.

"Just keep spreading that monster yarn," Pearsoll was saying as the two men came within earshot. "You've got the whole country spooked."

Mahaffey chuckled. "Yeah, nobody will ever go near that canyon again . . . except us. And we'll be rich when we get through taking all the gold out of it."

Fargo's mouth tightened into a grim line. He had had his suspicions of Mahaffey, and now the man's own words had confirmed them. And to top it off, Pearsoll was mixed up in the scheme, too. That didn't come as a surprise to Fargo. From the start, he had pegged Pearsoll as no more honest than he had to be.

He might have stepped out of the alley and confronted them then and there, but again, fate took a hand. A man hurried from across the street and called softly, "Flynn."

Pearsoll and Mahaffey stopped as the man came up to them. "What is it, Farrell?" Pearsoll asked.

"I saw somebody go into the hotel a little while ago," the man said. Fargo recognized him as one of the hardcases who had been with Pearsoll when they clashed on earlier occasions.

"Well, spit it out, damn it," Pearsoll snapped when Farrell drew out delivering the news.

"It was that fella, Fargo, and guess who he had with him?" Farrell hesitated, then went on before Pearsoll could get irritated with him again. "The old man's granddaughters."

"What?" Mahaffey exclaimed. "Are you sure it was them? The boys and I saw the Apaches grab them a few days ago, while we were on our way out to the canyon."

Fargo felt a fresh surge of anger as he listened to the conversation. So Mahaffey, Jessel, and Luman had witnessed the capture of Glory and Vangie by the Apaches and hadn't done a damned thing about it. That showed how low-down they really were and didn't come as much of a surprise to Fargo. It explained, too, why Mahaffey was claiming that the two young women were dead. He had assumed that Rafaelito's warriors had killed them. It was a reasonable assumption.

"Sure I'm sure," Farrell was saying. "It was them. Ain't no mistakin' those pretty little hellcats. They looked big as life an' twice as tasty."

"Son of a bitch!" Pearsoll said. "I was hoping they were dead."

Mahaffey said, "I don't see that it makes any difference. The old man abandoned the claim."

"Not officially, he didn't. He could come back later and try to say those diggings are rightfully his."

"Wouldn't make any difference," Mahaffey insisted. "There's no law around here, nobody he could squawk to."

"Maybe not right now, but you know people have been pushing for Congress to make Arizona a territory all its own. We get a territorial government in here, that'll mean courts and laws, and Olmsted's liable to say whatever gold we took out of there really belongs to him." Pearsoll rubbed his jaw in thought. "I figured that with those girls dead, the old man would head back wherever he came from, as soon as he was able to travel. Now that we know the girls are still alive, it might be better to just get rid of all of them."

Mahaffey said, "Wait a minute. You're worried about Olmsted suing us, or something like that, but you're willing to just kill the three of them."

"You never know what a damned judge will do," Pearsoll said, "but dead is dead, and no court can do anything about it."

The other two men couldn't argue with that. Pearsoll's position was ruthless but simple and effective.

"What about Fargo?" Farrell asked.

"He strikes me as the sort of hombre who sticks his nose in where it's not wanted," Pearsoll said. "We might ought to get rid of him, too, but let's take care of the old man and the girls first."

Mahaffey caught at his sleeve as he started to turn away. "What are you going to do, just march into the hotel and kill them?"

"It's too late to get water in your guts now, Mahaffey. You didn't say a damn word when I took that ax to Luman and Jessel, and they were supposed to be your pards. If the lode in that canyon is as rich as it's supposed to be, it's worth three more killings."

"All right, all right," Mahaffey muttered.

"Anyway, we won't kill them here in town. We'll grab the girls and tell the old man to get his wagon and drive out like he's leaving. Then we'll meet him somewhere out away from the settlement and kill all three of them. We dump the bodies in a gulch somewhere, and the buzzards will take care of the rest. If anybody ever finds the bones, there won't be anything to connect them to us."

"Yeah, I guess. Somehow I never thought it'd be like this, though."

"You want to be rich, you've got to do whatever it takes," Pearsoll said.

Fargo had his hand on the butt of the Colt. He had heard more than enough and was ready to step out of the shadows and challenge them. The odds would be three to one against him, but he planned to down Pearsoll first. With Pearsoll dead, Fargo didn't think the others would go through the attempt on the lives of Olmsted, Glory, and Vangie. Besides, there was a good chance he would get them, too, before their bullets put him down.

Before the iron could slide out of leather, though, a boot scraped in the dirt behind Fargo. He started to turn, but he didn't make it before something crashed into the back of his head. A brilliant explosion behind his eyes blinded him, and he went spiraling off into darkness . . . a darkness from which he might never return.

The first thing Fargo was aware of when consciousness began to seep back into his brain was the stinging of splinters against his skin as he lay with his face pressed to a rough board. The pain helped wake him up even more. He felt the boards bouncing a little under him and gradually realized that he was lying in the back of a wagon.

His shoulders ached because his arms had been jerked behind him and the wrists lashed together. His feet were tied, too. He was trussed up so tightly he couldn't move very much. But he was able to lift his head a little. He peered out through slitted eyes.

It was still dark, but the moon was low in the western sky and almost full, so it gave plenty of light for him to be able to see Olmsted, Glory, and Vangie. They were sitting with their backs against the sideboards of the wagon, and from the way their arms were pulled back, Fargo knew their wrists were tied together behind them. Their heads were down, and an air of despair hung over them.

The conversation he had overheard from the alley next to the assay office came back to Fargo. He knew that Pearsoll and Mahaffey had put their plan into action. They had kidnapped Glory and Vangie somehow and used them as leverage to force Olmsted into leaving Gila City in the wagon. Now the plotters had all of them, and Fargo knew all too well what fate Pearsoll and Mahaffey had in mind for them.

His head pounded painfully. He must have been out cold for quite a while if Pearsoll and Mahaffey had had time to capture all four of them. Over the creaking of the wagon wheels and the plodding hoofbeats of the team, Fargo heard other horses moving along beside the vehicle. He lifted his head a little more and saw Pearsoll and Farrell and another man riding alongside the wagon. Mahaffey was on the seat handling the reins. Fargo's eyes narrowed even more as he squinted at the fourth man. His teeth ground together in anger as he recognized the rider's prominent, outthrust jaw.

Richmond, the man who ran the assay office. The son of a bitch was in on it with Pearsoll and Mahaffey, Fargo thought.

Well, that made sense. There was no one better to have tipped off Pearsoll to the riches in Skeleton Canyon than Richmond. Pearsoll and Mahaffey had probably been on their way to the assay office from the Pine Tree Saloon when Fargo had spied on them. And likely it had been Richmond who had spotted him in the alley and clouted him on the head. It all came together in Fargo's brain . . .

But knowing the truth didn't do a damned thing to loosen those bonds around his wrists.

Olmsted, Glory, and Vangie hadn't noticed that Fargo was awake, and neither had their captors. Fargo let his head sink again, turning it so that his face wouldn't be pressed so painfully against the splintery boards of the wagon. He kept his breathing deep and regular, as if he were still unconscious.

And he began working on the rawhide thongs that bound his wrists behind his back.

Whoever had tied him up had done a good job of it. The thongs were so tight that his fingers were half-numb. He struggled to twist his hands back and forth and get a little play in the rawhide. When he was finally able to move his hands slightly, he began using his fingernails to claw at the skin of his wrists. If he could start some blood flowing, that would dampen the rawhide and make it stretch some. Getting loose that way would be a long, tedious, painful process, but given enough time it might work. Fargo figured it would take the rest of the night and part of the next morning to reach Skeleton Canyon. That might be enough time.

If that was where they were headed. Pearsoll and his fellow plotters might decide to stop and kill them before they ever got that far.

After a while, Pearsoll and Richmond began talking together in low tones. By listening hard, Fargo could make out the words.

"Fella's got a reputation," Richmond was saying. "Folks call him the Trailsman. When word gets around that the monster killed even the famous Skye Fargo, people will never come around that canyon again."

So they *were* going to Skeleton Canyon, Fargo thought. Since they had been able to grab him, they had decided to take advantage of the opportunity to reap even more benefits from their phony monster yarn.

Pearsoll laughed. "We'll chop 'em all up into little pieces, all right, but be sure to leave enough so they can be identified."

From the wagon seat, Mahaffey said, "What about those Apaches? They're liable to come back and try to kill us. They don't like people being around that place."

"To hell with those savages," Pearsoll said. "I left word for the rest of the boys to follow us. Once they get there, that canyon will be so well defended that the Apaches won't bother us."

Fargo wouldn't have bet on that. The way Rafaelito

felt about Skeleton Canyon, the war chief would probably attack no matter how many hardcases were inside the canyon. Pearsoll and the others were fools.

That was what happened, though, when gold was involved. Men lost all their common sense and couldn't think about anything except getting their hands on as much of the shiny metal as possible.

Fargo liked money. A man had to have it to buy whiskey and to play cards, and those were two of his favorite things. But he worked for whatever he had, and he had never been tempted to steal it from anyone else. Nor could he understand the lure of great riches. As long as a fella had enough, why would he need more?

Of course, one man's definition of enough might be different from another man's.

Fargo thought about that as he continued struggling to loosen the rawhide thongs. His movements were slow and deliberate, carefully designed not to attract any attention. He felt a bit of wet warmth on his wrists now and knew he had scratched the skin enough to draw a little blood. The problem was that he could no longer feel his fingers at all. He needed to get his hands loose soon enough so that he could work some feeling back into them before he had to go into action.

Farrell edged his horse closer to Pearsoll's and asked, "What about them girls, Flynn? We gonna have some fun with them before we kill 'em?"

"Damn it," Pearsoll said. "Once you got your share of the gold, you can buy yourself all the whores you want, Farrell. Keep your mind on what's important here."

"Yeah, yeah," Farrell muttered. He didn't sound happy about it, though.

Fargo wondered if there would be any way of playing the hardcases against each other. There probably wouldn't be time for that, but he would keep it in mind anyway, in case the opportunity presented itself.

The wagon rolled on, and after a while, Mahaffey glanced back and said, "I don't think Fargo's ever going to wake up. You must've stove in his skull when you hit him, Richmond."

"If he's dead, so much the better," the crooked assayer replied. "That'll just make it easy to cut him up like the monster did it."

"What about that monster?" Farrell asked worriedly. "There ain't really such a thing, is there?"

Pearsoll laughed again. "Of course not. It's just a legend. I heard about it from an old Apache a year or two ago. Never really thought anything about it, though, until Richmond told me about the gold the old man found in the canyon. That's when I started figuring out a way to use the story to make everybody steer clear of the place. We'll clean out all the gold and then won't even go back to Gila City. We'll head for California instead. It may be years before people forget about the monster and go back to Skeleton Canyon. We'll be long gone by then."

And to accomplish that goal, Fargo thought, all Pearsoll had to do was brutally murder Luman and Jessel. If he and Olmsted and the girls died, too, that would bring the total of victims to half a dozen. That was nothing to a man like Pearsoll, especially when compared to a fortune in gold.

Farrell wasn't satisfied. "You said something about the skeleton that gave the place its name," he prodded. "What happened to it?"

"From the looks of things, Fargo and the others must've buried it." Pearsoll snorted. "I don't know what else could be in that grave. Damn fool thing to do, if you ask me. Those old bones weren't hurting a thing. They should've just left 'em alone."

Fargo was beginning to think the same thing. He didn't really believe in curses, but it did seem like he had been jinxed ever since he had discovered the skeleton in the cave. He was still alive, though, and that counted for a lot. He wasn't going to give up until he was dead, and if there was any way to keep on fighting after that, he would.

He twisted his wrists a little harder, trying to stretch the rawhide. Now that he thought about it, he didn't have as much time as he had believed at first. Once the sun came up, Pearsoll and the others would be able to see the blood on his wrists and would guess that he was awake and attempting to free himself.

And already the sky was getting gray with the approach of dawn, which he saw when he risked a look through narrowed eyes. He had maybe another hour to work at it.

Olmsted snored. The old-timer had fallen asleep, despite the desperate situation in which he found himself. Glory and Vangie looked awfully tired, too. They hadn't gotten that long sleep they wanted, or the hot bath. They still wore the tattered clothes they had been wearing since leaving the Apache camp.

The wagon rolled on. Fargo had enough slack now in the rawhide thongs that he thought he might be able to slip his right hand out. He worked his fingers, slowly opening and closing them, and they tingled painfully as blood flowed back into them. He wasn't sure what he would do when he got his hands free. He though he could lunge up from the wagon bed and grab Mahaffey from behind. Then he could use Mahaffey as a shield while he snatched the claim jumper's revolver out of its holster. The odds would still be high against him, but even a slim chance was better than none.

Fargo wasn't going to get even that chance. The crack of a rifle suddenly split the early morning air, and nearby a man grunted loudly. "Son of a bitch!" Pearsoll yelled. "Farrell's hit!"

Fargo jerked his head up off the planks, knowing that nobody was going to be looking at him now. He saw Farrell topple out of the saddle, blood spurting from his throat where a bullet had torn it out.

"Oh, my God!" Mahaffey howled. "It's the Apaches!"

11

It was, for a fact. Fargo saw the muzzle flashes from several rifles as ambushers fired from behind rocks on both sides of the trail. He ripped his hands free from the rawhide thongs, taking off still more hide in the process, and rolled toward Olmsted, Glory, and Vangie. "Get down!" he shouted at them. He reached up, grabbed the girls, and hauled them down until they were stretched out flat in the wagon bed. Olmsted bellied down, too, taking advantage of the cover offered by the thick planks of the wagon's sides. Bullets thudded into the boards.

Mahaffey yelled and flapped the reins and sent the team lunging ahead. He hunkered low on the seat, making as small a target of himself as possible. From horseback, Pearsoll and Richmond returned the fire, banging away with six-guns. Fargo didn't figure they would do much damage in the poor light, but they weren't going to give up without a fight.

Fargo understood that. Surrendering wouldn't do any good. The Apaches would kill all of them, and probably slowly and agonizingly, at that.

"Head for the canyon!" Pearsoll roared at Mahaffey. "They won't follow us in there!"

That canyon had served as a refuge more than once, but Fargo didn't think they would reach it this time. From the glimpses he got of the surrounding landscape, they were still several miles from Skeleton Canyon.

The Apaches would probably close in on them before they could get there.

It was their only chance, though, so Mahaffey whipped the team mercilessly and kept the wagon bouncing and careening along the trail. Pearsoll and Richmond galloped alongside the vehicle, twisting in their saddles to throw lead back at the bushwhackers. Fargo thought Richmond rode sort of funny, hunched over in the saddle, and he decided that the assayer had also been hit in the initial volley, though not as seriously as Farrell, who had likely been dead when he hit the ground.

Considering everything, though, they had been lucky to lose only one man in the ambush. Now they were out of the trap and fleeing for their lives.

Fargo's feet were still tied. He twisted around while still lying flat in the wagon and worked at the knots. Now that he could feel his fingers again, he made some progress, though the knots were stubborn and it would have been faster to cut the thongs with a knife. He didn't have one, so he settled for untying them, and in a few minutes he was able to loosen the bonds enough so that he could kick his feet free.

"Stay down," he grated to Olmsted, Glory, and Vangie. Then he crawled toward the front of the wagon and lifted himself behind the seat. He called to Mahaffey over the pounding of hoofbeats, "Give me a gun!"

Mahaffey let out a startled yell and jerked his head around to see Fargo. He let go of the reins with his right hand and reached for his gun. Fargo's fingers clamped around his wrist. "Give it to me!" Fargo urged. "I'll help you fight off the Apaches!"

Four men stood a better chance than three, and Mahaffey knew it. He said, "Take it!" and turned his attention back to handling the reins. Fargo reached down and plucked the revolver from the holster on Mahaffey's hip.

He turned toward the back of the wagon and threw

himself down as a bullet sizzled past his head. He crawled to the tailgate and raised himself enough to look over it. In the growing light of day, he saw a dozen or more Apaches pounding after them on horseback. Apaches seldom used horses in their attacks, preferring to fight on foot, but that didn't mean they couldn't ride well when they had to. They were closing in quickly.

Pearsoll and Richmond pulled ahead, urging more speed from their mounts. "Damn it, don't leave us!" Mahaffey screamed at them, but the two men ignored his frantic plea. They were more interested in saving their own hides. They probably thought the Apaches would stop to kill everyone in the wagon, and that would slow down the pursuit.

Fargo sighted carefully over the tailgate and squeezed off a shot. He was rewarded by the sight of one of the horses in the forefront of the pursuers suddenly collapsing as if its legs had been jerked out from under it. The rider screamed as he was thrown through the air. The horses right behind the one Fargo had shot couldn't avoid a collision, and there was a sudden pile-up as a couple of the animals went down. More screams sounded in the dawn as men were crushed by thousands of pounds of horseflesh or had flesh torn and bones shattered by flailing hooves.

The Apaches dropped back, but Fargo knew they wouldn't be slowed down for long. He turned back to the seat and said to Mahaffey, "Give me a knife!"

This time Mahaffey didn't argue. He pulled out a clasp knife and fumbled it into Fargo's hand. Fargo opened the blade and quickly went to work on the rawhide bonds on the hands and feet of Olmsted, Glory, and Vangie.

"More guns!" he called to Mahaffey.

The claim jumper reached down to the floorboards and then passed back another revolver and a Henry rifle. Fargo recognized them as his own weapons. He pressed Mahaffey's revolver into Olmsted's hands and told the old-timer, "Make every shot count." Then he asked Glory and Vangie, "Which one is a better shot with a handgun?"

"I am," Vangie said, and Glory nodded in agreement. Fargo gave her his Colt and kept the Henry himself. He handed Glory the knife. If it came down to a hand-to-hand fight against an Apache warrior, Glory would have no chance, but at least if she was armed, she might be able to force them to kill her quickly.

A glance told Fargo that Pearsoll and Richmond had pulled well ahead of the wagon by now, and the gap was increasing all the time as they raked their horses with their spurs. Fargo's eyes narrowed. He would deal with those two later . . . if there was a later.

Then he turned toward the back of the wagon, levered a round into the rifle's chamber, and lifted the Henry to his shoulder. The Apaches were coming on again. He drew a bead as best he could in the wildly bouncing wagon and started firing.

Some of his shots went wild, but several of them knocked warriors off their ponies. Olmsted and Vangie added to the fire and got lucky a time or two as well. Fargo began to think that the Apaches might decide to turn back. They were paying a high price for their attack.

Mahaffey yelled in alarm. Fargo looked around and saw that the wagon was approaching a bend in the trail. The turn was a sharp one, and at the breakneck speed they were going, the wagon would never make it. Mahaffey pulled back on the reins, trying to slow the team. To the left, the ground dropped off in a steep slope to the Colorado River. If the wagon went over, it would probably roll all the way to the water.

Abandoning the wagon at this speed was dangerous, but staying with it was sheer suicide. "Jump!" Fargo shouted at Olmsted, Glory, and Vangie. They looked scared out of their wits, but they clambered onto the sideboards and leaped out into space, away from the drop-off.

Fargo hesitated. "Mahaffey, let's go!" he called to the claim jumper.

"I can make it!" Mahaffey shouted back without looking around. "I can make it!"

Fargo knew he couldn't, but it was too late to argue. The Trailsman stepped up onto the sideboards and pushed off.

He sailed through the air and then slammed into the ground. The impact knocked the Henry out of his hands and the air out of his lungs. Breathless, stunned almost into unconsciousness, Fargo rolled over and over on the ground, and as he did so he was vaguely aware of a great, rending, crashing sound that filled the air, punctuated by the shrill screams of horses. He came to a stop on his belly, and for a few moments it was all he could do to lie there, gasping and clinging to awareness.

He heard the thud of hoofbeats around him, and when he was finally able to look up, he saw half a dozen Apaches on horseback surrounding them. One of them, he saw in the glare of the newly risen sun, was Rafaelito.

Fargo waited for the rifle in the war chief's hand to belch lead and flame and end his life. Instead, Rafaelito lifted the barrel of the weapon and motioned for his warriors to do the same.

"You are ready to die," Rafaelito said in Spanish.

Fargo looked at him coldly. "Few men accept death willingly, but I do not fear it."

"Then fear this." Rafaelito smiled, but his eyes were just as icy as Fargo's. "It has been decided. The only way to appease the Old One is to give him those who disturbed his bones. If he takes his vengeance on you, he will leave our people alone."

Fargo knew what Rafaelito was getting at, and a familiar chill went through him.

They were going back to Skeleton Canyon, and whatever it was that lurked there.

Olmsted, Glory, and Vangie had been badly shaken up by their falls when they abandoned the wagon, but they didn't have any broken bones. By the time all of them had been put on ponies and had their hands tied again, Fargo's brain had cleared and he was trying to figure out some way to turn this situation to their advantage.

They were alive, and that was damned lucky, he thought. It was more than Mahaffey could say. Fargo had seen the claim jumper's body lying in the wreckage of the wagon beside the river, his head twisted at an impossible angle on his shoulders. The wagon had busted to pieces, and the horses were all dead, some of them having been dispatched by the Indians.

The group rode toward Skeleton Canyon. Pearsoll and Richmond would already be there, Fargo suspected. That was the only safe place for them in this sweeping wilderness.

Or was it safe? Everybody who ventured into that gloomy defile seemed to die sooner or later. . . .

But everybody died sooner or later, Fargo reminded himself. It was the price of living.

As they rode along through the brightening day, Fargo found himself between Glory and Vangie. He indulged his curiosity and asked them, "How did Pearsoll and the others get hold of you back in town?"

"We decided we wanted that bath before we turned in," Vangie said. "We were on our way down to Giddings's place when they jumped us."

"The bathhouse wasn't open that late," Fargo pointed out.

"We figured Giddings would open up for us," Glory said.

"We can be pretty persuasive when we want to," Vangie added.

Despite the seriousness of their situation, Fargo

149

chuckled and shook his head. He could just imagine . . . only he didn't have to, having sampled the charms of both women for himself.

In a quiet voice, Glory said, "Skye, what does Rafaelito plan to do? He won't just let us go, will he?"

"He says he's going to give us to the monster."

"But there's not really a monster . . . is there?" Vangie asked.

"Pearsoll killed Luman and Jessel," Fargo explained. "Used an ax on them to make it look like something had torn them up. That was part of the plan to scare people away from the canyon. I reckon he and Mahaffey were partners from the start, or pretty close to it, anyway. They've been out to run the three of you off, or kill you, ever since Richmond told them about the gold you'd found."

Olmsted was riding behind them, close enough to hear the conversation. "And to think I trusted that bugger," he said bitterly.

"Richmond seemed trustworthy enough," Fargo said. "You never can tell what the lure of gold will do to a man, though."

It was midmorning when Skeleton Canyon came into sight. Fargo expected Rafaelito and the Apaches to ride right up to the canyon, but they stopped half a mile short of the opening in the cliffs. "We will wait for night," Rafaelito announced. "That is when the Old One walks."

Fargo didn't mind the delay. He hoped it would give them a chance to escape. But as the heat of the day grew and the blazing sun traveled through the sky overhead, the warriors watched the prisoners like hawks. Fargo, Olmsted, Glory, and Vangie had no choice but to sit on the sandy ground, in the shade of some rocks, and wait.

No one bothered to feed them, though the Apaches let them drink from water skins. By dusk, Fargo was about as tired and hungry as he had ever been. He couldn't remember the last time he'd had a decent sleep and some food.

He looked toward the canyon and wondered if Pearsoll and Richmond were in there. It was pretty likely they were, Fargo decided. That was where the two men had been headed. Had they seen the Apaches? Did they know they were trapped in the canyon?

As darkness dropped over the wild, rugged landscape, the Apaches prodded the prisoners onto their feet at rifle point. "Walk toward the canyon," Rafaelito ordered.

Fargo started walking. Olmsted and the girls followed him. As Fargo saw it, this decision by the Apaches was a lucky break for them. Even though he and the others were unarmed, he would take his chances with Pearsoll and Richmond.

The warriors followed them, but not too closely. They began to hang back even more as the group approached the mouth of the canyon. Finally, Rafaelito called out, "Stop." Then he surprised Fargo by adding, "We will leave your weapons here."

Fargo turned and watched as the war chief placed the Henry and the two revolvers on the ground, along with Fargo's Arkansas Toothpick. The heavy-bladed knife must have been recovered from the wreckage of the wagon. Rafaelito and his men backed away.

"You wonder why I return your weapons to you," Rafaelito said, as if he had read Fargo's mind. "It does not matter. Steel and lead will not save you from the Old One. He will take his vengeance on you and leave the Apaches alone." When the Indians were far enough away, Rafaelito motioned for the prisoners to come forward and reclaim the guns and knife.

They did so, Fargo giving the Henry to Olmsted this time and holstering his Colt. Vangie had the other revolver. Fargo handed the Arkansas Toothpick to Glory. "This is a bigger knife than the last time," he said. "Can you handle it?"

"If I have to," she said, but she didn't look too confident. None of them did.

Fargo turned toward the canyon and said, "Let's go."

The moon had not yet risen, so there was only starlight. The mouth of the canyon was a gaping black maw in the cliffs.

Were Pearsoll and Richmond right inside, drawing a bead on them? Fargo didn't know, but he hoped the darkness would conceal them effectively enough to prevent that. Their feet crunched on sand as they walked up to the canyon.

To his surprise, Fargo saw a faint glow coming from around the bend. Pearsoll and Richmond were here, all right, and they had built a fire in there, deep in the canyon. He paused and glanced back. He couldn't see the Apaches now, but he knew they were there and would likely open fire if Fargo and his companions tried to turn back. There was nothing they could do except go ahead.

Fargo marched into the canyon. Olmsted, Glory, and Vangie followed him.

A few minutes later they came to the bend and went around it. The flames of a small campfire were clearly visible now, as were the shapes of the two men sitting beside it. Pearsoll must have heard them coming, because he stood up quickly, turned toward them with a rifle in his hands, and called out, "Who's there? Answer me, damn it, or I'll shoot!"

"Hold your fire," Fargo said.

"Fargo!" Pearsoll exclaimed. "I thought the Apaches got you!"

Fargo noticed that Richmond hadn't gotten up. The assayer still sat by the fire, hunched over with his arms pressed to his midsection. Fargo had thought that Richmond was wounded during the fight that morning, and his attitude now seemed to confirm that.

"The Apaches did get us," Fargo said.

"Us?"

"Olmsted and the girls are with me," Fargo said.

"The Apaches let you go?" Pearsoll sounded like he couldn't believe it.

"They sent us in here to be killed by the Old One," Fargo explained. "We're sacrifices, I guess you could say."

Pearsoll laughed harshly. "So they think the monster's goin' to eat you, is that it?"

"You don't believe in the Old One, Pearsoll?" Fargo asked. "You wanted everybody else to believe there was a monster in this canyon. That's why you murdered Luman and Jessel, dug up that grave, and left that shackle out where somebody would find it."

"Killing Luman and Jessel was a small price to pay to keep everybody away from the gold," Pearsoll said. "What happened to Mahaffey?"

"Dead. He broke his neck when the wagon crashed, while we were trying to get away from the Apaches."

Pearsoll shrugged. "No great loss. He whined too damn much. And Richmond's dyin', too. Got a bullet in his guts, so I figure he'll be gone by morning. Then the gold will be all mine."

Olmsted said, "You're nothin' but a dirty claim jumper!"

"It's not jumping a claim," Pearsoll said, "when the man who first claimed it is dead." He jerked up the rifle.

"Get down!" Fargo called as flame bloomed from the muzzle of Pearsoll's gun. The bullet whined away as Fargo went to a knee and palmed out the Colt. He squeezed off two fast shots. One missed, but the other clipped Pearsoll on the left arm. The hardcase was jerked halfway around by the impact. He cursed and flung more lead at Fargo and the others. Then he ducked out of the firelight as they began returning his shots.

Richmond finally stood up, stumbling forward with his left arm pressed to his belly. His right hand fumbled out his six-gun, and he shouted incoherent curses as he came toward them, firing wildly. Fargo aimed as best he could by starlight and the flickering glow of the flames and put a bullet in Richmond's chest. The slug drove the crooked assayer backward and dropped him to the ground by the fire. He twitched a couple of times and then lay still.

Pearsoll was out there in the darkness somewhere, unseen and still plenty dangerous.

Fargo took cartridges from his belt loops and reloaded the empty chambers in the Colt's cylinder. Then he said quietly to Olmsted and the young women, "Stay here. I'll see if I can find Pearsoll."

He moved forward, skirting the fire so that Pearsoll couldn't get a good shot at him.

He had played this sort of deadly cat-and-mouse game before, hunting an enemy in the darkness at the same time the enemy was hunting him. The threat of the Apaches remained outside the canyon, but for now, Fargo couldn't worry about them. He had to deal with Pearsoll.

"Fargo!" Pearsoll shouted. The way echoes bounced off the canyon walls made it difficult to tell where he was. "Fargo, listen to me! You got some of it wrong! I never dug up that grave. All I did was scatter the rocks. I never messed with any shackle, either. I don't know what the hell you're talking about!"

Fargo frowned. He didn't believe Pearsoll . . . but what reason did the man have to lie about that?

"Maybe there is a monster in this canyon!" Pearsoll continued. "Maybe it's sneaking up behind you right now. Look out, Fargo!"

Two things happened suddenly. Fargo figured out why Pearsoll was yelling at him, and at the same time Fargo caught a whiff of the same musty odor that had filled the cave, the smell that he thought of as signifying death. Pearsoll's shouts were meant to cover up the sounds he was making as he slipped through the darkness toward Fargo. His powerful shape loomed up out of the shadows as he lunged at the Trailsman.

Fargo hadn't fallen for the shouted warning. He

hadn't turned around to look for a monster behind him, because he knew a killer was coming at him from the front. Starlight winked on the blade of the knife that Pearsoll thrust at Fargo's chest. Fargo tried to twist aside.

He didn't have time to get completely out of the way. The razor-sharp blade sheered through Fargo's buckskin shirt, but it clanged against something and was stopped before it penetrated flesh. Fargo smashed his left fist into Pearsoll's face and knocked the hard-case backward. Pearsoll cursed as he dropped the knife and grabbed his revolver from its holster.

Twin bursts of gun flame licked from the muzzles of the weapons. Fargo felt the disturbance in the air next to his ear as Pearsoll's bullet went past him. Pearsoll grunted under the impact of lead and stumbled to the side. His gun drooped. He tried to bring it up again but failed. Fargo fired again. This time the bullet jerked Pearsoll's head back as it bored through his brain. He folded up, limp in death.

Fargo reached inside his shirt and pulled out the shackle that had been around the skeleton's wrist. His fingers felt the small notch where Pearsoll's knife had struck it. Somehow, the shackle had kept the blade from penetrating Fargo's chest.

As he stood there, the musty odor grew stronger. It smelled like a snake, only much stronger. Fargo grimaced at the stink. He wanted to get away from Pearsoll, away from this whole damned canyon. He tossed the shackle behind him and stalked toward the fire.

Something scuttled away behind him. Fargo stopped, glanced over his shoulder, but didn't see anything. Some sort of small animal, he told himself. Maybe a lizard or something like that.

He walked on and called out to the others, "It's over! Pearsoll's dead!"

Olmsted, Glory, and Vangie met him at the campfire. "What do we do now?" Olmsted asked. "Do you reckon Rafaelito is still out there?"

"Let's take Pearsoll's and Richmond's horses and find out," Fargo said.

"You don't think we should wait until morning to leave?" Glory asked.

Fargo looked back at the stygian depths of the canyon. "I've had enough of this place," he said. "I'd rather take my chances with the Apaches."

As it turned out, Rafaelito and the rest of the warriors were gone. They must have heard all the shooting in the canyon and figured that no one would come out of there alive, Fargo thought. Either that, or they believed that anyone who survived had been blessed by the spirits and should be left alone. All Fargo really cared about was that no one bothered them as they rode out of the canyon and headed for Gila City.

It was a long, slow trek, riding double on the two horses, but they finally reached the settlement after dark on the next day. The hotel clerk had put the Ovaro in the stable and had held rooms for Fargo and the others. Fargo didn't do much of anything for the next couple of days except sleep and eat, but at the end of that time, he was ready to ride on and resume his journey to California.

"You're not going back to Skeleton Canyon, are you?" he asked Bert Olmsted before he left.

"Good Lord, no!" the old-timer exclaimed. "After everything that's happened, the girls and I want no part of the bloody place."

Bloody place, Fargo thought. That was a pretty good description, even though he knew Olmsted hadn't meant it exactly that way.

He wasn't sure whether to believe Olmsted or not. But six months later, he looked across the room in a Barbary Coast saloon and saw Olmsted's familiar skinny figure, dressed now in expensive finery rather than a desert rat's rags. The old Englishman was flanked by a pair of gorgeous, exquisitely gowned young women, one blond, one brunette. Glory and

Vangie were prettier than ever. When they saw Fargo, they greeted him with squeals and hugs and kisses. The next twelve hours or so got pretty passionate . . . and pretty tiring.

But it was a mighty good tired that Fargo felt as he sipped whiskey and smoked a cigar with Olmsted at a table in the saloon the next day. "Did you go back to Skeleton Canyon?" the Trailsman asked.

"Certainly not. We went on up the river and found an even more lucrative strike in another canyon . . . one that wasn't cursed."

"Glad to hear it." Fargo tossed back the rest of his whiskey. "Anybody ever see that monster again?"

"No. But people still don't go near Skeleton Canyon unless they have to." Olmsted paused, then added, "The army killed Rafaelito in a little skirmish a couple of months ago."

Fargo grunted. In a way, he was sorry to hear that. He had felt some respect for the war chief. Rafaelito had been doing what he thought best for his people, trying to protect them from a danger that, according to Apache legends, had come down through the ages.

Fargo had been busy in the months since he had seen Olmsted. But in odd moments, he had wondered if Pearsoll had been telling the truth, there at the last. If Pearsoll hadn't dug up that grave, who had? If Pearsoll hadn't dropped the shackle on the ground where Fargo had found it, who had?

"I say, Fargo, you don't believe there really *was* something . . . well, something unearthly in that canyon, do you?" Olmsted asked.

Fargo smiled. Some questions just didn't have answers.

Not good ones, anyway.

LOOKING FORWARD!
**The following is the opening
section of the next novel in the exciting
Trailsman series from Signet:**

**THE TRAILSMAN #277
HELL'S BELLES**

*Hell's Canyon, the Northwest, 1861—
Where human devils hunger for female flesh,
and a savage angel
named Fargo serves them only lead.*

Skye Fargo had been following the women for nearly two days, trying to decide if they were crazy, drunk, or just hog stupid.

Close observation, however, finally made him conclude they were the greenest greenhorns he'd ever seen. And some of the shapeliest, all five of them. But they obviously had no concept whatsoever of the danger they were in.

An attractive, auburn-haired gal in a rose taffeta dress drove their celerity wagon, a lighter, cheaper version of the popular Concord coach. And she was doing a piss-poor job of it, Fargo told himself. She literally didn't know gee from haw.

No way in hell did she get that four-horse rig this deep into the gold-rich mountains of the Northwest without a guide who knew scouting and trail craft. Which might explain the male snakebite victim Fargo had buried just east of here in the rugged Bitterroot Range.

The man some called the Trailsman wasn't sure of the exact calendar month and didn't need to be, any more than he needed a watch. The slant of the sun told him the time, the bite in the air the season. He had headed far west just after the first big snowmelt, when the passes were no longer blocked by ice. Nights in the Rockies were still knife-edge cold, days that bracing kind of cool that almost tempted Fargo to shave off his beard just so he could feel the air stinging his cheeks.

He had crossed the Wind River Range through Jackson Hole and over Teton Pass. He then continued west over the dangerous Lolo Trail, used by the Nez Percés when heading east to hunt buffalo on the plains. Riding into the pristine beauty of the Northwest at this time of year was a natural tonic to Fargo. Another reason he had wandered out this far was to see if his old hunter and trapper friend Snowshoe Hendee was still above the earth.

But spotting the female-filled celerity wagon had diverted Fargo's attention and hooked his curiosity. For the past twenty-four hours the women had made no effort to leave their ill-chosen campsite in the Seven Devils Mountains beside the Snake River. And the reason was obvious: a snowmelt-swollen river ahead, and no trails behind that they could manage. They were trapped.

This was no country for a conveyance of that size, even in the hands of a capable teamster. The mania for establishing new roads and ferries, which Fargo saw sweeping much of the West, was frustrated this far north by long winters with temperatures reaching forty below zero. And the only "settlement" (so new that word was a stretch) was the overnight tent city of Lewiston, well north of here. The few roads just recently begun by the U.S. Army were abandoned as the gathering drumbeats of sectional warfare back East drew soldiers off the frontier.

Right now, though, Fargo noticed with sudden interest, four of the women didn't seem to have one damn care in the world—except for braving the shockingly brisk water of a mountain-runoff stream as they disrobed and plunged in for a bath.

"Now, at this point," Fargo remarked quietly to his Ovaro, "a gentleman would turn his gaze away."

A few seconds later, a grin tugged at Fargo's bearded lips. "Ain't no gentlemen west of Omaha." He kneed the pinto stallion forward for a better look at this free flesh show.

"Oh, my stars and garters, it's *frigid*!" cried out a petite beauty as she poked one toe gingerly into the burbling stream.

She wore only a muslin chemise tied off all the way up over her alabaster fanny, which glowed, in the afternoon sun, like fine ivory. The thick russet thatch covering her mound was a shade darker than the hair worn in a single braid over her left shoulder. She began to untwist the braid.

"Shoo, Tammy, you're just a little priss," teased a tall, leggy blonde with a trace of a Swedish accent in her musical voice.

She had long, pale-gold hair, long-lashed eyes of lavender blue, prominent Scandinavian cheekbones. Even less inhibited than Tammy, she had stripped buck. Fargo was forced to shift in his saddle as he took in those long, shapely legs, the taut little strawberries-and-cream caboose, the corn-silk bush and firm, high breasts with nipples turned into hard little bullets by the crisp spring breeze.

To cap the climax, she had an identical twin who was wading in right behind her, likewise naked as a newborn. Only now did Fargo spot one sure way to tell the twins apart. This second sister had a little crescent-shaped birthmark on her curvaceous right hip.

The pearly allure of the twins' skin was an exciting contrast to the flawless mocha flesh of the fourth woman who had wandered down to the stream to bathe. Fargo, who had been to New Orleans a few times, had already guessed she was most likely Creole, a mixture of French and Spanish blood. A pretty, fine-boned face with coffee-colored, wing-shaped eyes, all crowned by raven-black hair in coronet braids.

She had stripped down to her red satin corset and was idly unlacing it with one hand as she advanced, engrossed in a book.

Fargo rode to the edge of the screening timber, then reined in and swung down, leaving his brass-frame Henry in the saddle boot. Since graze was scarce and the Ovaro hungry, he put the stallion on a long tethering rein so he wouldn't wander into view of the women. But the hearty Ovaro, never spoiled by stall-feeding, was content to stand still and browse the juicy pine needles lying about.

"Girls, just *listen* to this," the Creole lovely called to her companions, her accent more French than Southern.

In a melodramatic stage style, she began reading aloud from her book. Fargo hadn't crept quite close enough yet to see the title, but the author's name was Washington Irving.

" 'With his horse and his rifle, he is independent of the World, and spurns all its restraints.' "

Just as she mentioned spurning restraints, the Creole sighed audibly and wiggled out of her corset. Fargo admired her unblemished skin, the color of sunlit amber. In his vast experience, very few women could move with such catlike grace while bare naked—a fluid, seamless motion except for the swaying of impressive breasts.

"Hooboy! Right there's your problem, Yvette," Tammy taunted the Creole in a hill-country twang Fargo guessed was west Arkansas. "You're alla time lookin' for men like in them silly storybooks. *Hee*-roes, my sweet aunt! And you going on twenty-four years old? You best grab you a meal ticket before your tits drop. Just be happy if you can find one that can last more'n a minute in the saddle."

While Tammy delivered this sage advice, Fargo watched her bend forward from the grassy bank to suds and rinse her hair. The petite little hill girl's luscious butt yawned invitingly wide at Fargo, bold as the crack of day. The leggy twins, meantime, were lathering each other's backs, shivering and exclaiming at the cold. The fifth woman, the auburn-haired one who seemed to be in charge, remained up at the campsite.

For Fargo, it was a true embarrassment of erotic riches. But even now, when any red-blooded man under eighty had a damn good excuse for relaxed vigilance, Fargo's old survival instincts took over. These silly cottontails might not realize it, but danger surrounded them from several sources.

Still sheltered in dense brush, he reluctantly averted his gaze from the frolicking nymphs to closely study the surrounding terrain.

He was in the wild region east of the Blue Mountains and west of the Bitterroot Range, with Lewiston several days' ride to the north and the Boise River well south, just before the desolate lava-bed country began. Vast Hell's Canyon sprawled straight ahead of him, split by the Snake River. The canyon was aptly named. Ancient glacier scars pitted the landscape and made travel, especially by vehicle, truly hellish.

The area looked pristine and deceptively peaceful, at first glance. He watched the low, gliding swoop of an eagle searching for prey. Spruce forests and other conifers turned the surrounding slopes bluish-green, and at the higher elevations pure-white aprons of snow still clung to the granite peaks and rock plateau above the tree line.

Just then Fargo's concentration was momentarily broken by a feminine shriek. But it was only a chorus of jeers from the bathers. The twins were teasing Tammy for being afraid to enter the ice-cold water.

" 'Hang your clothes on a hickory limb, but don't go in the water!' " they chanted in unison. "That's fraidy-cat Tammy!"

"Oh, serve it on toast," Tammy retorted. She popped open a pink parasol to protect her fair skin from freckles while the wind dried her dark russet hair.

By now the twins were playfully wrestling over a lump of lye soap. Fargo, hot blood pulsing in his veins, watched their bodies grind together until they fell in a giggling, thrashing heap of bare limbs and perky bottoms. Yvette, apart from the others, stood in water up to her thighs, a dreamy expression on her face as she sudsed herself in slow circles as her thoughts roamed far afield.

Fargo somehow forced his attention back to the surrounding terrain. It *looked* peaceful, all right. But this stretch of the Northwest had lately become a tinderbox. It began in 1858 with a major gold strike up north along the Fraser River in British Columbia. Then gold was discovered throughout this stream-rich area in 1860. Violence and lawlessness were widespread and inevitable given two undeniable facts: Gold was why men were here, and whatever they found, or robbed, they carried with them.

But bad as all that was, Fargo had noticed another source of festering tension: White prospectors were staking out tomahawk claims—girthing trees to kill them and mark their diggings. Problem was, they were staking their claims on forbidden Nez Percé reservation land.

In past years Fargo had been cordially received at the Nez Percé village nearby, on the Clearwater fork of the Snake. But in the last few days he'd seen signs that several local tribes were especially busy knapping flints to make arrow points—plenty of them.

So it was finally time to confront these pretty tenderfeet with the truth. Either they lit a shuck toward civilization, and in a puffing hurry, or they were marked for carrion bait—if not worse.

"Don't be scared, ladies," Fargo called to the startled beauties as he stepped out into the open. "The name's Skye Fargo. I'm a mite rough-looking and ripe from the trail. But I'm lovable as a newborn kitten."

He flashed a toothy smile as he touched his hat to the shocked women. Their separate reactions were telling—and quite promising.

The twins stood exposed but modestly cupped their hands over their breasts. Yvette, the Creole beauty, plunged her entire body under water up to her neck. But she couldn't pry her eyes off the new arrival. Tammy, her honey-colored gaze sparking to life at sight of this tall, buckskin-clad interloper, stood up boldly. She wanted him to see all of her petite but alluring body. The sheer, wet muslin was nearly transparent and nicely emphasized the plum circles of her nipples.

Tammy was also the first to recover from the surprise. She flashed Fargo a kittenish smile. "Well, ain't *you* the sassy one, Mr. Skye Fargo?"

"Sassy as the first man breathed on by God," he assured her. "Only, not *quite* so pious."

Yvette, Fargo noticed, had wasted her time by trying to hide in the crystal-clear mountain water—her lithe, lovely form was clearly visible. In fact, a fish always looked bigger underwater—and so did a set of high-grade tits.

"*M'sieur* Fargo, your eyes!" she exclaimed. "Right now I feel that I am gazing into a bottomless blue lake high, high in the mountains. You *are* the rugged frontier type just like Captain Bonneville, *mais oui.*"

"Don't know the gent," Fargo apologized. "Cavalry?"

"Oh, don't mind her, Mr. Fargo," Tammy said. "Captain Bonneville is the hero in a storybook she's reading. Yvette fancies herself an actress from New Orleans, thinks you can eat ideas and swap dreams for cash."

Tammy's man-hungry eyes feasted on Fargo. "But me? I'm Tammy Lynn Jones from Fort Smith, Arkansas, and I don't find my men in books. Them silly blondes gawking at you is the Papenhagen twins from the Nebraska sand-hill country."

"I'm Hilda," said one of the twins.

"I'm Helga," said the other, the one with the crescent birthmark.

"Hilda, Helga, pleased to meet both of you."

Right then, however, Fargo realized the little skinny-dipping party was about to come to a screeching whoa. The auburn-haired woman had spotted him and was hurrying down the slope from their camp, her face a sternly pretty mask.

"That's Mattie Everett," Tammy supplied quickly. "Sorta in charge of us. Nice enough sometimes, but pushy and likes to get on her high horse."

"Sir, what *are* you doing here?" Mattie demanded as she drew up in a huff. "Hilda, Helga! Shame on you two! Get some clothes on! You, too, Yvette and Tammy. You girls are acting like Santa Fe harlots."

She was a few years older than the other women, Fargo noticed, and like them a damn fine looker. There was also more worldly experience in those pretty brown eyes than her high-hatting manners let on. And it wasn't a corset, he realized, that gave her the hourglass waist and flat stomach. His eyes lingered there, picturing her naked.

"I also have a face," she told him sarcastically.

"Yes, ma'am, and *it's* mighty easy to look at, too."

What were the odds, Fargo thought idly, that on the woman-scarce frontier, all five of these gals would just happen to be pretty and fetchingly built? Hell, most men out here were grateful for any female with a few teeth left.

"Mattie, this is Skye Fargo," Tammy put in quickly.

"May I ask why you're here, Mr. Fargo? Or would that question be too obvious, given the bare flesh surrounding you?"

"Good thing I am here," Fargo assured her. "*Some*body has to watch over you pretty pilgrims. No offense, Mattie, but you gals are so green you didn't even think to find the lee side of the cold night wind when you camped last night. Hell, a rabbit has that much sense."

Angry red spots appeared on her cheeks. "Watching over us? Just plain watching us, you mean."

"Well, I've already confessed to the others how I wasn't Bible-raised," Fargo admitted in a hale, cheerful tone. "Matter fact, Mattie, I'm a pagan pure and simple. But when I see prime ladies like all of you, I *do* believe in heaven. And, angel? I'm not looking away from a naked goddess unless she tells me to."

"My stars!" Tammy exclaimed. "Not only a randy stallion, but a charmer, too. First dibs, girls."

Mattie whirled toward Tammy and the others, fists balled on her hips. "Push those thoughts right out of your mind, Tammy Lynn. We're *all* spoken for already, and we've even signed contracts. Say, didn't I tell you girls to get dressed? And as for *you*!"

She turned back toward Fargo, eyes blazing. "You're still staring at them?"

"Why, hell, yes. Nobody's told me to stop."

"Stop!"

Fargo grinned amiably. "Sure—soon as you put it to a vote. I'm a true democrat, and the rest don't seem so offended as you."

Mattie sputtered some angry retort, but Fargo missed it. He had been watching an eagle hovering and gliding out over the Snake. Only, at the moment it was veering sharply to the west, flying full-bore away from the river.

Moments later, several crows did likewise.

"Excuse me, ladies, I need to take a quick squint around. I suggest you get into less, ahh, exposed locations. Hope we can resume this little chat shortly."

Fargo headed back toward the thick stand of brush and jack pine where he'd left the Ovaro. His plan was to ride in a wide loop, then scout the riverbank on foot.

"Nobody asked you to come back, Fargo!" Mattie called after him. "Donner Summit was fifteen years ago. Progress has come to the West since then. We don't need your so-called help."

Without looking back, Fargo opened his mouth to reply. But from the direction of the river, a rifle spoke for him.

The high-caliber report cracked like a giant blacksnake whip, echoing throughout the canyon in a hundred explosions and spooking the team horses up at camp.

There was no dramatic cry of pain, no arms flung skyward as if in angry protest at dying. As the horrified women watched, Skye Fargo's legs simply folded like empty sacks and he flopped to the ground hard, face-first. He lay there stone still—except for the gruesome sound of his toes scratching the dirt in several quick, jerky death twitches.